Caster & Fleet M

THE CASE OF THE FATEFUL LEGACY

PAULA HARMON
LIZ HEDGECOCK

WHITE RHINO BOOKS

Copyright © Paula Harmon and Liz Hedgecock, 2019

All rights reserved. Apart from any use permitted under UK copyright law, no part of this publication may be reproduced, stored in a retrieval system, or transmitted, in any form or by any means, electronic, mechanical, photocopying, recording or otherwise, without the prior written permission of the copyright owners.

This is a work of fiction. Names, characters, businesses, places, events and incidents are either the products of the author's imagination or used in a fictitious manner. Any resemblance to actual persons, living or dead, or actual events is purely coincidental.

ISBN-13: 978-1094951065

For Elizabeth Garrett Anderson
physician and suffragist

Chapter 1
Katherine

'Appy berfday!' exclaimed Bee, waving her cup vigorously, 'Uxes and trumf!'

'Ray! Trumf!' agreed Lucy, waving with a little more decorum but not enough to stop her party hat from slipping over her eyes. Aunt Alice hastened to right it, and somehow managed to give her daughter a cuddle in the process.

'Happy birthday, James and Lucy!' bellowed Albert. 'To success and triumph!'

The drawing room at Hazelgrove was bright. Extra lamps had been brought in to lighten even the darkest corners. The red velvet curtains, closed to defend against the cold November dusk, glowed like ruby wine. Around the blazing fire sat James's mother, his sister Evangeline, Albert and Connie, my cousin Moss and Aunt Alice. The two little girls sat on stools and cheered.

James leaned across and whispered. 'How many times

can they all say the same thing?'

I giggled. His party hat was awry too, rakish over his left eye. 'Why not?' I said. 'There's plenty to celebrate: two birthdays, the paper doing so well and the small matter of the Caster and Fleet Agency managing to fathom ten small and two large mysteries in eighteen months, despite distractions like Connie having another baby. This last case really was a "trumf". I was worried we wouldn't puzzle it out before Christmas, but Connie had brainwave after brainwave. If she has a third child, she'll be solving things before they've happened.'

Six-month-old George was dozing on Moss's lap, jerking his little arms every time the girls shouted. Uncle Moss had been nervous of children until Bee was old enough to walk to him with a picture book and demand a story. Since no one argued with her apart from James, Moss had complied and never looked back. She had insisted he came to the party, even though her own birthday wasn't for another month. Connie now joked that if her nursery staff gave notice, she'd know where to find a replacement. But Moss's freedom was safe for the moment. The redoubtable Nanny Kincaid sailed into the room with junior nurses Lily and Hannah in her wake like a small invading flotilla intent on capture.

'Come along, everyone,' said Aunt Alice, lifting Lucy from her stool, 'it's bedtime.'

'Is it?' whispered James into my hair. 'How lovely.'

'Shh,' I admonished, 'behave.'

'Yes,' said Connie, taking George from Moss's arms. 'Time for sleep.'

Spotting Bee's mutinous glare, James's mother chipped in. 'I do believe Uncle James's old toys are in the nursery, being very naughty. They need a little girl to show them how to behave. I shall go and see.' She rose and held out her hand for Bee.

'Uncle Moss and Auntie Angeline too,' said Bee.

'Just to the bottom of the stairs,' said Moss.

The flotilla, complete with captives, sailed out of the room.

Albert, having kissed his offspring goodnight, settled in an armchair. 'At last,' he said.

James rang for champagne.

'If Lucy and Bee can manage to celebrate without champagne,' I argued, 'why can't you and Albert?'

'Just because it makes *you* feel sick, K,' said Albert. 'I don't see why I should suffer.'

I blinked at him. 'Who told —?' I turned to James. He shook his head. Surely Connie had kept my secret.

'No one told me,' said Albert. 'I'm just observant. Caster and Fleet are not the only ones who can do detective work.' He closed his eyes and pressed his fingers to his temples. 'I deduce . . . five months along.'

'How?'

'Ah,' said Albert, opening his eyes and grinning. 'No denial I see. You forget that I, as a father, am vastly experienced in these things. Let me count the ways. One: two months of you looking green at Simpson's finest cuisine, which has recently been replaced by you ordering extra helpings for the first time in your life. Two: falling asleep in the music hall during the most exciting bits.

Three: the barely-discernible but just-about-perceivable alteration in a figure which until now has been somewhat scrawny.'

For the first time ever I wished crinolines were in vogue. I could have gone all the way to confinement without people being sure. Perhaps. I felt my face flame and restrained the urge to run a hand over my stomach which bulged a little under the fullness of my skirt. It didn't help that for the last hour, I'd had a peculiar internal fluttering sensation, like a tiny fish flicking its tail inside me.

'If he's inherited any of your tendencies, K,' added Albert as if reading my mind, 'he'll be a fine kicker.'

'How do you know it'll be a boy?'

'James has grown a beard.'

'It's the style.'

'Well, it worked for us,' admitted Albert, running his hand over his unfashionably clean-shaven face. 'Hence George. But I've accepted the next baby will have to be a girl. Connie couldn't bear the scratchy kisses.'

'Had you men thought of joining James's father and Uncle Donald in the billiard room?' I countered.

'It's much more fun watching you squirm,' said Albert.

Fortunately for me Moss and Evangeline returned to the room at that moment. Moss wore a quizzical look on his face as if pondering some deep thought. It took me a moment to realise he wasn't staring into space but at Evangeline, and she was smiling because she knew Moss was looking at her. How very interesting.

'I think it was a bit noisy for Papa,' said Evangeline. 'And I imagine Mama will retire early; she's worn out from our visit to old Miss Quinton this morning. It's exhausting having holes picked in anything you do. I don't know how someone at death's door can manage such belligerence, but she does.'

'Miss Quinton's always been fond of you,' said James. 'She can't stand me.'

'You're a filthy man like Papa, that's why.' Evangeline winked. 'Your sex is the source of all human misery and nothing will be right until there's a woman prime minister.'

'My word,' said Moss. 'I hope we don't get a prime minister like Miss Quinton. There would be a revolution.'

Connie returned to the room just as the champagne was brought in. 'Aunt Alice and Mrs King are staying in the nursery,' she said. 'Nanny is a little affronted that her routine is not being adhered to, but it turns out the toys need a great many stories and . . . what's happening?'

'K's cat is out of the bag,' said Albert, patting the sofa for her to join him. 'Or rather, we know there's a cat in the bag ready to come out in a few months time. Or maybe cats. Who knows, it could be twins.'

'Albert!' Connie went redder than anyone in the room. She turned to me. 'I didn't —'

'I know,' I said. 'We may have to add Albert to the team. He's very skilled.'

Albert puffed out his chest smugly. Then his smile wavered a little. 'I say, K...' He glanced at James. 'Do you think perhaps you should... You do tend to throw yourself into your cases... Could you not both say the agency hasn't any capacity for a year?'

'No!' said Connie and I together.

'Don't waste your breath, Albert,' said James. 'Half the reason I insisted on having the party here was to get Katherine away from the office, the telegraph boy, the postman and that wretched telephone. Why did I let you talk me into it?'

Albert looked sheepish. 'I thought it would save cab fares if Connie and K could gossip on the telephone instead of meeting every five minutes.'

'You're both fussing about nothing,' I said, as James's father and Uncle Donald entered the room. 'I've never felt fitter, and the new case is mostly research and can wait till Monday. Besides, Reg is holding the fort.'

'Yes,' said Connie, 'let's get on with celebrating.'

'Ah, champagne!' said Uncle Donald. 'And peace and quiet. It's a shame your father couldn't be here, Katherine. I do so love our conversations.'

'It is,' I said. 'But his cough is only just —'

James's mother entered, bearing a telegram. 'I'm so sorry if this spoils the atmosphere, but we've had a message to say Miss Quinton has died in her sleep. A blessed release of course, she has been unwell for so long, but I have to say I wasn't expecting it yet.'

'Never mind, Mama,' said James. 'She's no longer suffering so at least you needn't worry about her any more. Especially as there's always good news to take the edge off the bad. Take a glass of champagne and — perhaps sit down. Katherine and I have something to tell you.'

CHAPTER 2
Connie

'At least it's out in the open,' I said, gazing at the Berkshire countryside rolling gently past the window. 'I wondered how long it would be before I slipped up.'

'I'm impressed.' Albert, who was taking full advantage of the legroom in the carriage, grinned at me. 'Two — three months? And not a word, even to me.' He leaned down and murmured in my ear. 'I shall never play cards with you, Connie. Not for money, at least.'

'Oh, do be quiet.' I turned my head to kiss him. 'It isn't often we get a little time to ourselves these days. Let's enjoy it before the bustle of the train.'

Even at close range, Albert had changed little from the tall, slim young man I had met four years earlier on a trip to the Museums. While he had lost much of the awkwardness which had characterised our first meetings he was still slender and dark-haired, and his eyes were as blue as the day we had met. As usual, he had slept soundly the previous night, though in a strange bed, while I had lain awake for some time, worried that Bee's late bedtime would affect her.

I had been proved right in the morning, when I visited the nursery to find a very cross Bee and a grim-faced Nanny. 'I've done my best with Miss Beatrix's hair,' she said, 'but she would not sit still for me.' Her use of Bee's Sunday name reminded me of my mother. 'She was whispering and giggling with Miss Lucy half the night.'

'I am sorry to hear that, Nanny,' I said. 'Has she had her breakfast?'

'After a fashion,' said Nanny.

'Have you had yours?'

'Yes, ma'am.'

'In that case, it is probably best that you start for home. Lily, can you enquire about getting the trap out. There is a train for London at ten o'clock.' I paused. What had I forgotten? 'Oh! How is George?'

'Jojo seepin,' said Bee, pointing to the cot where, indeed, George was sleeping, thumb in mouth and eyes squeezed tight shut.

'He woke up for his morning feed, had a little play, and off he went again,' said Nanny Kincaid.

'I think he takes after his father,' I remarked. 'Not that Albert sleeps with his thumb — oh never mind me.'

'I'll go and see about the trap,' gabbled Lily, and hastened from the room. Nanny Kincaid permitted herself a small smile.

'Are you sure you'll be able to manage them both on the train?' I asked.

'Oh yes,' said Nanny, stooping to retrieve a valise from under the bed. I had a feeling she might have rolled her eyes while she was down there. She put the case on a chair, unbuckled the straps, and began to transfer neatly folded clothes and napkins and muslins into it.

'I'll let you get on, shall I?' I said to her bent head, and made my exit.

Katherine had made an excellent breakfast, aided by James's mother, who sat beside her and offered a little more toast, some marmalade, perhaps another cup of tea, until Katherine pushed her chair back with a look of determination. 'I couldn't eat another morsel, thank you.'

'Perhaps you should have a little rest,' said James's mother. 'You could use the drawing room or the library, or go to bed.'

'Honestly I'm fine, Mama,' said Katherine, smiling at her. 'I've just eaten a little too much.'

'Nonsense,' said James's mother, 'you may eat as much as you like.' And she put her hand gently onto Katherine's stomach.

Katherine's eyebrows shot up. 'Perhaps I shall go and lie down in the bedroom,' she said. 'James, would you mind…?'

James glanced up from his plate of ham and eggs. 'Of course, dear,' he said, and helped Katherine to her feet. 'Connie, you are the guardian of my plate till I return. Don't let Albert snaffle it.'

I saluted. 'Yes, sir!' James made a face at me and took Katherine's arm.

***

A loose stone in the road jolted me back into the present. 'When do you think K will start taking it easy?' asked Albert.

'If she doesn't have a choice, I imagine.' I laughed, but my heart wasn't in it. 'I'd buy a ticket to see her face if she's put on bed rest.' I remembered my own unwilling compliance, my restlessness, and the utter boredom of confinement. 'James will do his best.'

'Of course he will,' said Albert, laying his hand on mine. 'Although he's dashing around on his own account rather, too.'

'These newspaper magnates, you see…' We were all proud of the success of *The Worker's Voice*. In eighteen months it had grown from a free sheet given out at temperance meetings and workers' rallies to a halfpenny publication sold in its own right. The *Voice*, as we called it for short, had also broken several news stories which were picked up by papers including the *Chronicle* and the *Manchester Guardian*. Lord Marchmont, according to James, had indicated his gracious approval.

'True.' Albert considered. 'I suppose if he's holed up in editorial meetings then at least he isn't getting himself into trouble in slums and dockyards.'

'And you've never been bashed on the head in the course of duty,' I retorted.

'Only when you drag me into trouble, darling.' Albert leaned over…

'Anyway,' I said, half-laughing at his comical disappointment, 'the Kings are staying on at Hazelgrove another day at the behest of James's parents — soon to be grandparents. So Katherine will have to rest.'

'If she isn't attempting to matchmake,' said Albert. 'I saw K eyeing my brother and Evangeline last night.'

'Oh. Oh dear.'

'I know. I buttonholed Moss in a quiet moment and told him to stop gazing at Evangeline if he didn't want to be teased.'

I stared at him. 'You didn't.'

'Not in so many words. But Moss is a diffident sort of chap, and any hint of a nudge will send him running the other way. Speaking of running —' The carriage slowed unexpectedly and Albert grabbed my arm as I shot forward. 'We'd better hurry if we're going to catch the next train.'

***

By the time we arrived home I was ready to drop. The train had been late, overfull, noisy and dirty, and I felt a little seasick. 'Next time James proposes a party at Hazelgrove,' I said in the cab, 'remind me to talk him out of it.'

'It's only once in a way,' said Albert, who had slept for most of the journey, and as a result looked annoyingly fresh.

'Once might be enough,' I said darkly. 'I just hope the children had a better journey with Nanny.'

Johnson opened the door to us. 'Welcome home sir, ma'am.' He helped me off with my coat and handed it to Violet as she bustled up.

Albert laughed. 'Anyone would think we'd been around the world. Good afternoon, Johnson. What have we missed?'

Johnson's mouth twitched. 'Just a few calls, but everyone left cards. Your post is on the salver, as usual.'

'Excellent, thank you. Dinner at the usual time?'

'Yes, sir. The children arrived two hours ago and are having some fresh air at the park.'

'Oh good,' I said. 'Hopefully that will shake the train fidgets out of them.'

'The train fidgets,' said Johnson. 'Very good, ma'am.' He began to retreat. 'Oh! I almost forgot. A telegram came for you earlier, ma'am.' He edged to the salver and handed me the familiar yellow envelope, then retreated to a safe distance.

'None for me?' said Albert. 'I feel rather left out.'

'Ssh.' I broke the seal with my thumb and smoothed the paper.

At end of tether STOP do not reply STOP will tell you myself STOP be prepared V

'What is it?' asked Albert, peering over my shoulder.

'I'm not entirely sure,' I replied. 'It isn't a case, if that's what you're worried about.'

'I'm worried that you look worried,' he said. 'Who's it from?'

'The only *V* I know who might wire me is my sister Veronica. But I don't know what she's at the end of her tether about.'

'Would you like to freshen up, ma'am?' said Violet, picking up my carpet-bag.

'Yes, I'll come up in a moment,' I replied absently, going to the salver and sorting through its contents. 'Cards from Alexandra and Delia . . . an invitation . . . ooh, a letter from Maisie Frobisher . . . here we are.' I picked up a fat, pale blue envelope covered in my sister's handwriting in its scrawliest form. I guessed that she must have posted it herself, for Mother would never have allowed such a scruffy missive to leave the Swift household. Even the stamp was crooked. 'Well, I suppose I'm about to find out.' I wiggled my finger under the flap, and —

Someone banged on the door.

'Perhaps Veronica's here in person, to save you the trouble,' said Albert, stepping out of Johnson's way.

But when Johnson opened the door Bee burst through it, followed by Lily. 'Oh, Miss Bee!' scolded Lily.

'What has she done?' I asked, bracing myself.

'She wouldn't come away from the pond, ma'am, so I said I'd bring her home while Nanny had another turn with Master George, and she let go of my hand in the street and ran!'

'Oh, Bee...' I crouched down and looked seriously at my panting daughter, who looked back at me and giggled. 'I don't know what you're laughing about, Beatrix Lamont. You're in trouble.'

'Mama funny!' cried Bee.

The doorbell rang, a long insistent ring, and Johnson sprang to answer it. I sighed. 'Take her to the nursery, Lily. We've had a long day. I'll come up shortly.'

'Connie! I'm glad you're home.' Veronica rushed to embrace me then stopped short. 'Just off the train?'

'Um, yes, actually.'

'Thought so. I'll go and pay the cab.' Veronica whisked off and returned a minute later carrying a carpet-bag of her own, and followed by a puffing cabman with two suitcases. 'Did you get my letter?'

'Yes, but I haven't had time to read it yet. What on earth has happened?' My sister, while flushed and slightly breathless, didn't seem particularly distressed.

'It's Mother. She's been driving me potty for weeks, and she's gone too far this time. So I thought I'd come and stay with you. You don't mind, do you?'

I opened my mouth to reply, without any sense of what I would say to her, and the telegraph boy's double knock sounded.

'Veronica, can you go and make yourself comfortable in the drawing room, please?'

Veronica shot me a look. 'Will there be tea?'

'Eventually.'

She swept off with rather bad grace and I took the envelope which Johnson, with an apologetic look, handed to me.

Please could you return to Hazelgrove Mon pm STOP Something odd re Miss Q STOP Will meet you at station STOP K

I glanced up from the paper and caught sight of my blank, tense face in the mirror, covered in sooty smears. No wonder Bee had laughed. But right now, laughing was the last thing I felt like doing.

14

Chapter 3
Katherine

Hazelgrove felt rather empty after the Lamonts had left. It was absurd, of course. There were still five Kings, three Framptons and a houseful of servants, but without the children and a hint of romance, all the bustle had gone and everything was subdued. My parents-in-law, whom I'd long called Mama and Papa, seemed both relieved and sad that the house was quiet. The Framptons would be returning to London with James and me on Monday morning.

'I really do think you should send your Father here,' said Mama as we finished lunch. 'London can't be good for his cough. It's a most unhealthy place. In fact…' She bit her lip as she hesitated. Before she could suggest I stayed for the next four months if not years if not decades, I excused myself from the table and asked Evangeline if she would like to take a drive with me in the autumn sun. Mama beamed approval and patted my hand. We escaped before she could tell us how many layers we should put on.

With the tiniest push from Evangeline, I climbed with only a little difficulty into the trap, picked up the reins, clicked to the pony and took a deep breath of clean, cold air. It became a white cloud when I exhaled. I didn't feel as if I'd swallowed poisoned glue: it was a definite improvement on London fog. Perhaps I should send Father out to recuperate. After all, he *was* sixty-four.

I wondered why Evangeline was fidgeting and realised she was suppressing laughter. 'Whatever's the matter?'

'Mama has been clucking round you so much, and you've been looking more and more as if someone has tied your leg to a post.'

'Oh dear, is it that obvious?'

'Only to someone who understands.' Evangeline sobered a little. She was thirty-three, yet until my marriage two years ago she had barely left their house, let alone the small village of Hazeldown. Since then, apart from a few visits to us in Bayswater, little had changed.

'Shall we go out of the grounds?' I suggested.

After a pause she nodded. 'Does James know you're driving the trap?'

'He's the one who taught me,' I pointed out. 'And we're hardly racing. I'm fairly sure I can walk faster than Blossom.' The pony whinnied and flicked her head as if she'd heard, but maintained her slow amble as we passed through the gate. 'Anyway, James won't fuss if he knows what's good for him. Where shall we go?'

Evangeline pondered. 'Would you mind going down this lane?' she said at last. 'I'd like to pay my respects to Miss

Quinton. I said I'd go with Mama later, but she won't mind. Miss Quinton's staff were so fond of her. Well, the maids were. It's hard to imagine her companion Miss Taplow is fond of anything.'

'I sense that you were fond of her, too.'

Evangeline smiled. 'She was rather a curmudgeon, but I suppose that's allowed when you're elderly.'

'Will her family be there by now?'

'She had none. Miss Quinton was quite alone in the world.' Evangeline tucked the blanket more firmly round both our knees. 'She was the only daughter of a man who thought she should be educated as well as a boy.'

'Was she able to do much with her education?'

'There was no outlet open to her. She travelled abroad a little when she was younger, but considered most of the Continent too hot and disorganised. I believe she kept journals but otherwise preferred facts and wanted a profession. Even Papa admits she would have made an excellent if terrifying judge. And of course most of the family money went to her cousin because he was male. Not that she need complain — she wasn't poor. This is her place.'

The elegant Georgian house was already firmly in mourning. A black bow had been tied to the door and when we were admitted by an elderly parlourmaid, the mirrors and pictures were shrouded in black muslin.

'I shall bring Miss Taplow directly,' murmured the parlourmaid, showing us into the chilly drawing room. Her eyes were red and her mouth quivering as if she were suppressing tears.

'Thank you, Hillbeam,' said Evangeline. 'I am terribly sorry to hear of your loss. I know how fond you were of Miss Quinton, and she of you. May I pay my respects to her?'

The parlourmaid shook her head and drew in her breath with a huge sob. 'It's disgraceful, that's what it is. And *she* didn't hardly do a thing to stop it.' Without explaining she withdrew, leaving us shivering.

A moment later a tall, spare woman entered. Her greying hair was pulled back so tightly that it must have been agony. Certainly the scowl on her face indicated temper rather than grief. 'Good afternoon Mrs King, Miss King,' she said. 'I have ordered that the fires need not be lit. There is no point in wasting money, is there?'

'I'm sure I don't know, Miss Taplow,' said Evangeline. 'I was so sorry to hear of Miss Quinton's passing. May I pay my respects to her?'

Miss Taplow drew herself up and with an even deeper scowl glared at the empty fireplace. 'I'm afraid not,' she said. 'The doctor was not satisfied and has taken her — her remains for a post-mortem. Most undignified. I tried to argue but of course he would not listen, and now the servants are being impossible.' She paused as if something had occurred to her. 'Of course, Miss King, your father is a man of influence and significantly more important than a village doctor. Perhaps you could prevail upon him to make Dr Stokes stop. I understand this wholly unnecessary procedure won't take place before Monday, so there is still time.'

'I make no promises, but I'll see what can be done,' said

Evangeline. 'Good-day.'

She was very pale as we drove back to Hazelgrove. 'That was wrong of me,' she said. 'Nothing can be done, can it?'

I shook my head. 'It's unpleasant, but it's a doctor's right. I doubt anything will come of it. She was eighty-two, you say.'

'Eighty-three.'

We drove in silence for a while. Something was nagging at me and I couldn't think what it was. Blossom's hooves clopped and the sun burst with a shaft of light from behind a cloud.

'Evangeline.'

'Mmm.'

'I know it's an odd question but I didn't quite catch the housemaid's name.'

'Hillbeam. It's a local name, but she's the only one I've met. Have you ever heard it?'

'Yes, and I'd like to send a telegram. Do you think we have time before they send out a search party?'

***

I met Connie at the station on Monday and Standish drove us to the house. All the way there she clasped our *Caster and Fleet* briefcase as if it were her own flesh and blood, refusing to let me take turns in carrying it in case of injury to my baby.

It wasn't until Standish opened the gates to Hazelgrove that she'd forgiven me enough to say, 'I'm just worried. You shouldn't be chasing cases.'

'I'm not,' I argued. 'If I were I'd have come home yesterday, grabbed the notes from the office, kidnapped you and come back on the afternoon train.'

'I still don't see what the hurry is. And you should be looking after yourself. Wait till you're on bed rest.'

'I hope not to be,' I argued. 'You weren't with George till the last month.' I sighed. 'Please don't be like everyone else, Connie, I want this baby very much and I won't risk that. At the moment I feel perfectly well but I promise that whenever I don't, I shall rest. Would you like to know a secret?'

'Another one?' Connie tutted and then leaned forward. 'Go on.'

'One of Margaret's lecturers — a female doctor — is doing research into pregnancy and childbirth. I'm one of her subjects. I couldn't be in better hands. Next time you're —'

'That's reassuring,' interrupted Connie, 'but no-one is experimenting on me even *if* I have another. Anyway, why the rush that isn't a rush? Mr Hillbeam asked us to find any relations, you've found a possible relation. Can't we finish the research in London or simply let him know what we've discovered?'

I shook my head. 'We need to speak to Hillbeam herself, discreetly. She's sixtyish according to Evangeline, too old for her family records to have been registered anywhere except a church, presumably the one in the village if she's Anglican. I could hardly rummage in them yesterday, and of course they might be in the chapel or a Roman Catholic church instead, but I don't think so. Evangeline said she'd heard there had been some kind of scandal with an older sister many years ago, but she's rather preoccupied.

They're all upset about the post-mortem.'

'It does seem unnecessary for an old lady, so I'm not surprised.'

'And after the funeral and the will-reading on Tuesday, the servants will disperse. Who knows where Hillbeam will go. We haven't much time. Besides —'

The carriage lurched over a pothole and the fluttering in my stomach started up again. I stroked it and restrained myself from talking aloud to comfort the little being inside me.

'Besides what?' said Connie.

'I don't know,' I confessed. 'Something's not right. I can feel it.'

Connie laughed. 'First your sense of smell intensified and now your sixth sense?'

I grinned ruefully and shrugged. 'The doctor may have been right to question her death. If so, maybe we can help with the investigation.'

'Even if no-one wants us to?'

'When have we ever worried about what people want us to do?'

Connie pursed her lips and peered out of the window of the carriage. It was a grey drizzly afternoon and evening was falling. The lights of Hazelgrove twinkled, bright and welcoming.

'Do you think this is a real case?' she said at last, and clasping the portmanteau ever closer, turned to me. 'Are you sure it's for us?'

I had never seen her look so overwhelmed.

CHAPTER 4
Connie

The more I thought about the possible case, the less I liked it. The possibility of a speedy resolution to Jonah's enquiry was one thing. An investigation, involving a possible murder in James's home village, was quite another.

'Let's wait and see what the post-mortem finds,' I said. 'For now, we can concentrate on Hillbeam.'

Katherine turned to me as the carriage slowed, and I could just make out the reproach in her eyes. 'It isn't like you to be so cautious, Connie,' she said.

'Sensible,' I replied. 'One thing at a time.' I thought of the situation at home and closed my eyes. At least I would have a few days' respite from that.

On Saturday Veronica, over tea and cake in the drawing room, had made it clear to me that she had no intention of going home that day. 'What, and face Mother? You must think I'm mad! Anyway, I told her before I left that she'd be lucky if she ever saw me again.' Veronica snorted and took another piece of cake from the stand.

I poured myself another cup of tea, adding a little less milk this time. 'Did you mention where you were going?'

Veronica stared at me with round blue eyes over her rapidly-working mouth. 'She wouldn't care,' she said, once she had regained the power of speech. 'She hates me. I'm the worst daughter in the world.'

'I thought I was!' I exclaimed.

Veronica looked injured. 'I'm sure it isn't true that you are,' I said, feebly.

'*She* thinks so, and that's what matters to her.'

'Never mind that right now.' I got up and rang for Nancy. 'Please could you bring my writing case, and wait while I compose a telegram.' Nancy bobbed and sped off.

I thought Veronica's eyes would pop right out of her head. 'You can't tell her where I am!' she exclaimed.

'As far as Mother knows, you could be anywhere,' I said, folding my hands in my lap. 'I'm not having her call the police or send out a search party. And if she hates you so much, she'll probably be glad of a break from you.'

Veronica took more cake, tucked her feet underneath her, and eyed me reproachfully as I composed the wire. 'No reply requested, please,' I said, handing the sheet to Nancy. 'Tell Johnson to go at once.'

From that point Veronica had flung herself into a sulk, sitting silent at dinner and turning her back on me in the drawing room afterwards. I had taken the opportunity to peruse the letter she had sent me, but could glean little from it save that her situation was utterly unacceptable and no-one should have to put up with it…

'Connie! You can't go to sleep!' Katherine gripped my arm, none too gently. 'We have to hurry or we won't get to Miss Quinton's today.'

The carriage had come to a stop outside Hazelgrove and the lights looked warm and inviting. Inside the house there would be comfort, and quiet.

'Shouldn't we go over the papers first?'

'There isn't time!' cried Katherine. 'We must go and see Hillbeam. You stay here.' She opened the door of the carriage and scrambled down. 'Standish, can you take Mrs Lamont's trunk into the house, please? I'll hold the horse.'

'No you won't!' I nearly fell out of the carriage in my haste to stop her, but a footman was already on his way to help.

'I almost forgot!' said Katherine, making for the house. 'We need Evangeline. I'll just go and fetch her.'

I opened my mouth to protest, then thought better of it. With any luck this Hillbeam would turn out to be the key to our case, Miss Quinton's death would be attributed to nothing more sinister than old age, and I could sleep easy in my bed that night, far from tiresome sisters, fearsome mothers, and recalcitrant daughters.

***

'This *is* an adventure,' said Evangeline, sitting up straight in the carriage.

'I'm glad you think so,' I said, perhaps a little sourly.

Katherine had re-emerged from the house after fifteen minutes towing Evangeline behind her. I estimated that at least ten of those minutes had been spent bundling Evangeline up against the cold, since she was so well-muffled in coat, cape, and comforter that she had to be assisted into the carriage. 'I do wish Father wouldn't fuss,' she sighed, as she subsided into the corner seat.

It was a short drive to Miss Quinton's square stone house. I imagined her as a pale, austere, uncompromising woman, like the architecture of her home. Perhaps she would have disapproved of the furbelow of a crape bow. Katherine knocked, and we waited.

Eventually we heard the shuffle of footsteps and the clanking of a bolt, and a red-eyed, sniffling woman opened the door just wide enough to see us all. 'Oh, Miss King,' she murmured, 'I'm so sorry, but Miss Taplow isn't at home.' She did not open the door any wider.

'That's quite all right, Hillbeam,' said Evangeline, an encouraging smile on her face. 'I've come to visit you. Do you recall Mrs King, who came with me the other day?'

Hillbeam peered at Katherine for some time. 'Yes, yes I do.' She turned back to Evangeline. 'But I'm not fit company for visitors, my dear.'

I could feel the energy radiating from Katherine. She stepped forward and opened her mouth to speak, but as she did so the clack of rapidly approaching footsteps made her pause.

A tall thin woman in a grey wool coat marched up, her mouth set in a grim line. 'Good afternoon Miss King, Mrs King,' she said, stopping a few feet away.

'What did he say, Miss Taplow?' From Hillbeam's stricken face, I gathered that this Miss Taplow's expression was tidings enough.

'I shall tell you shortly, Hillbeam.' Miss Taplow's eyes

darted towards us. 'Ladies, I am afraid that neither of us is disposed to receive visitors at the present time.'

'My friend and I would like to discuss an important matter with — Hillbeam,' said Katherine, waving a hand at the briefcase I was holding. 'We are acting on behalf of a client, in London.' Her tone was brisk, almost clipped, and I saw from the set of her shoulders that she was having difficulty holding herself in.

'A client? In London?' Hillbeam's eyes opened wide. 'I don't know anyone in London!'

'I appreciate that this isn't the best time to call,' said Katherine, all in a rush, 'but we were worried that if we waited you might have left. As the funeral is tomorrow —'

'No it isn't,' snapped Miss Taplow. 'That's what I've just come back from.'

'The funeral?' Evangeline looked extremely confused.

'Yes,' said Miss Taplow. 'Putting it off, that is.' She sighed. 'I suppose you're as close to her as anyone was,' she said to Evangeline. 'Hillbeam, don't let Miss King stand there shivering any longer. Go and ask Cook to make tea.'

The parlour was scarcely warmer than the street, and the weak tea reminded me of Mrs Jones's early efforts. Nevertheless we sat together, Evangeline in an armchair, Katherine and I on one sofa, and Miss Taplow and Hillbeam on the other. Miss Taplow sat ramrod-straight, hands in her lap. Poor Hillbeam was perched on the extreme edge of her seat, wearing the guilty face of a pet which knows it is not allowed on the furniture and expects to be evicted at any moment.

'You, um, mentioned the funeral, Miss Taplow,' Evangeline ventured. 'Is it not to be held tomorrow, as planned?'

'It is not.' The words shot out of Miss Taplow. 'That interfering doctor sent a wire earlier and ordered it to be postponed.'

'Dr Stokes?' asked Evangeline.

'Full of his own importance,' she snapped. 'That man wants to make trouble. I never liked him.'

'Trouble?' Hillbeam's hands gripped the hem of her apron.

'The Reverend's not happy, I can tell you. Everything arranged to a nicety, and now Dr Stokes has said to postpone it without so much as a by-your-leave.'

'But why?' Evangeline looked puzzled.

'Some nonsense about more tests. Miss Quinton was in her eighties and anyone could see she wasn't well!'

Hillbeam put her apron to her face and wailed. 'My poor mistress!'

Katherine and I exchanged glances and rose. 'We're so sorry to have disturbed you,' I said. 'We'll see ourselves out.'

Miss Taplow rose too. 'That might be best,' she said. 'As you can see, Hillbeam isn't quite herself. It's been a trying time for us all.' She led the way to the hall. 'Perhaps if you call again in a couple of days, Hillbeam will be ready to talk to you about — the London matter,' she said to me. 'I shall try to persuade her.'

'That would be very kind of you,' I said, resolving to make sure that Miss Taplow was out of earshot when I did.

***

James's parents welcomed me back rapturously to Hazelgrove, and seemed to find nothing odd in my precipitate return. The warning bell rang for dinner before they had finished welcoming me, and I had to rush to make myself presentable for dinner.

Evangeline had looked thoughtful on the short drive to Hazelgrove, so much so that Katherine and I had refrained from discussing what we had just heard. She was in the same brown study at dinner, and her mother exclaimed at her quietness.

'That's what comes of going out in chilly November air,' Mr King said, wagging his head. 'She has almost certainly caught a cold.'

'I am quite well, Father,' said Evangeline, absently, and continued to push her fish around the plate.

The mention of wellness galvanised Mrs King, who cross-examined Katherine as to whether she might have caught a chill too, and suggested that perhaps she should go to bed soon, or at least retire to a sofa with an afghan, and would she like another helping of fish? Or perhaps she could have a larger helping of the beef when it came out. Katherine smiled and gently rejected her mother-in-law's suggestions, but I sensed she was rather glad not to have to discuss our call.

After dinner Mrs King suggested whist, and counting trumps and trying not to disgrace my partner kept me busy until bedtime. I was brushing my hair when a gentle tap sounded at the door and Katherine peeped in.

'Come in,' I said, laying my brush down. 'So, are you

content?'

Katherine frowned, and sat on the bed. 'Content with what, exactly?'

I faced her. 'Well, you felt something wasn't right, and you may be correct.'

She screwed up her face. 'Maybe, but…'

I raised my eyebrows. 'But what?'

'Well…' She rubbed her hands over her face, then leaned towards me. 'Did you see Evangeline at dinner?' she whispered. 'She looked — I can't describe it — but I'm worried about her.'

'In what way?'

'I'm not sure.' Her face was troubled. 'But I'm worried.'

Chapter 5
Katherine

I was used to the Hazelgrove night-time noises by now.

In London, from lamp-lit streets, came a constant rattle of wheels and clopping of hooves on metalled roads and footsteps on pavements — quick, spasmodic pattering feet that made you worry and the slow steady plod of the neighbourhood bobby that calmed you.

At Hazelgrove, I had once lain in pitch darkness straining my ears against what seemed to be utter silence. Then the noises started. Once they had unnerved me. Alone the first few times I'd visited, I'd stayed awake for ages wondering if those ghost stories about old houses were true. After my marriage, I'd cuddled into James's arms. Now I felt comforted when the old beams creaked, creatures scurried in the walls, soot fell down the chimney and somewhere outside a fox barked.

So I was no longer too nervous to creep along the landing and knock on Evangeline's door.

She was curled up in her chair by the fire, a pile of letters in her lap.

'Before you ask,' she said, 'they're from your cousin Moss.'

'I thought they might be.'

'Ever the detective.' She grinned and then sighed. 'I keep telling him to find a society bride, but he says it's me he wants. I just don't understand why.'

I sat on the opposite chair and reached for her hand. 'Because he loves you. If he'd wanted a society bride he's had plenty of time to find one. He's over forty.'

'Didn't he ever...'

I shrugged. 'I really have no idea without gossipy female relatives on that side to ask. And the men, especially Albert, are useless. But if you're what he wants and he's what you want, why worry? Do your parents know?'

'No,' Evangeline folded up the last letter and tied the bundle up. 'I think they suspect and they'd be quite happy. He writes openly once a month and via Norah once a week.' Her voice faltered a little. 'I don't want to live in London. I — I want Papa to teach me how to run things here. James doesn't want to come back. I could do it, I know I could.'

'Moss always says he'd like a place in the country, if that helps.'

'Does he?' Even by firelight Evangeline seemed to glow a little more.

'Be brave,' I said. 'If you love him, say so. Men find female subtlety completely incomprehensible.'

Evangeline giggled. 'Miss Quinton said it was because

their brains were less well formed in intellect and swollen with — er — animal urges.' Then she sobered. 'Papa says the inquest is tomorrow at eleven, and the funeral in the afternoon unless the coroner's court rules otherwise. Mr Innes the coroner knows us well, but he is rather cool towards Papa for arguing with Dr Stokes about the post-mortem.'

'Will you go to the inquest?'

'Goodness, no. Do you think the funeral will be awful? I've never been to one, yet Miss Quinton insisted Mama and I attend.'

This was unusual. 'Do you know who else has been invited?' I said.

'Only any other ladies who choose to attend,' replied Evangeline, who put on a severe voice. '"And there shall be no strong drink taken either before or after, nor the frivolity of funeral meats." No other ladies *will* go, of course. And then, strong drink or otherwise, I have been told I must attend the reading of the will. Katherine, would you come with me? I'd very much appreciate it.'

I nodded, but thought of how Connie had described the only funeral that she'd been to, and shuddered. At least this one would not be full of distraught loved ones, just acquaintances who would be glad when it was over. I wasn't sure which was worse.

As I returned to my own room along the dark landing, I put my earlier disquiet down to the peevishness of Miss Taplow and the barely constrained grief of Hillbeam. I felt annoyed with myself for dragging Connie all the way back, and didn't blame her for being irritated with me. Perhaps everyone was right and pregnancy did addle your brain. And as I lay awake in my bed, hugging the hot water bottle, my distaste for Miss Taplow faded. She was, presumably, a companion for want of a decent income of her own. She would soon be out of a home and out of work. I knew only half of that desperation — I had never been at risk of homelessness. Perhaps I was being unkind.

***

'Whatever happens, we'll be on the afternoon train,' I said to Connie as we rattled along in the trap. 'I've wired the men and they can collect us from Paddington at six p.m. And if you'd rather not come to the inquest, you needn't.'

'I don't mind that,' said Connie, holding onto her hat. 'Although it'll practically be over by the time we get there. I hope we've missed any discussion of innards. *Now* look at you — I thought you'd stopped feeling sick. Perhaps *you're* the one who shouldn't go.'

'I shall be fine,' I retorted, swallowing the sudden nausea and wondering if one could discreetly plug one's ears in public if necessary.

'What if the coroner does find something untoward?'

'Then we still go home. You were quite right, no-one has asked us to investigate and it has nothing to do with us. I'm sorry I pulled you away from all the troubles with Veronica.'

Connie let out a sigh. 'To be honest it was a good thing to leave her for two days. I was so cross.'

'Do you think there's an unsuitable young man behind all this?'

'Veronica?' Connie was startled. 'I'd be surprised. I can't see her settling for anyone less than very suitable and very very rich. Why do you ask?'

I shrugged. Now was not the time to discuss my own vague concerns about Margaret.

We had obtained all the evidence we could from the church register. I had found the record of Papa's christening. *Edwin Reuben James King, 3rd February 1828, son of Edwin King, Gent.*, and further down the same page *Keziah Hillbeam, 9th December 1828, daughter of Ebenezer Hillbeam, farm labourer,* and on the following page *Ruth Hillbeam, 30th October 1829.* It was the name our latest client Jonah Hillbeam had given us as his mother's. If we could ask some delicate questions of Miss Quinton's parlourmaid to be certain, the case would be closed and Jonah would have a family at last.

We slipped into the back of the coroner's court and found ourselves to be the only women there, apart from a neat young lady with a notebook, next to whom we were asked to sit.

'Are you press too?' she whispered. 'You've missed almost all of it, but I don't mind sharing. We female reporters must stick together.'

Before I could answer the man in front shushed us and, muttering about females, resumed his concentration on the inquest. Mr Innes the coroner was coming to the end of his summing up.

'And I direct that while Dr Stokes was being conscientious in trying to assure himself of the cause for heart failure, and may the court know —' his eyes sought out James's father, 'that it was perfectly within his right to do so, there appears to be no evidence to suggest anything other than advanced age brought about Miss Henrietta Quinton's decease. I direct that death was by natural causes, and that a certificate should be signed so that the funeral may take place without further delay or disrespect.'

I felt myself relax. Connie and I could go home with a clear conscience.

***

The funeral had been brief and bore little resemblance to the one Connie had described, being stripped to its bare bones, so to speak, and attended only by myself, Evangeline and her mother. Miss Taplow had, according to Evangeline, positively curled her lip in horror at the thought of going, and said she would stay at Lion House to await the solicitor.

Now I sat with Evangeline, holding her hand, in a dining room which felt even colder than outside. Evangeline's parents sat on her other side, and Miss Taplow on mine. The servants stood to one side though the solicitor, Mr Strutt, had indicated they were to sit.

The solicitor cleared his throat and surveyed us all.

'This is the last will and testament of Henrietta Elizabeth Annabelle Quinton, dated January 2nd 1894.'

Miss Taplow twitched. I saw her frown, and her mouth opened a little, then closed.

The solicitor continued through the document until he came to the crux of the matter.

'*To my companion and servants if they are still in my employ at the time of my death I leave the following:*

To Mary Taplow, one hundred pounds.

To Keziah Hillbeam, parlourmaid, a sum shall be invested to provide forty pounds per year for the remainder of her life.

To Agnes Booth, cook, fifty pounds.

To Sukey Black, housemaid, twenty-five pounds.

To Tessie Payne, tweeny, a sum invested to provide the means for ten years to enable her to return to school and thereafter train to be a teacher.

To Evangeline Dorothea King, provided she is unmarried at my death, the remainder of my entire estate including Lion House and 42a Wright Terrace, Primrose Hill.'

I could sense all the unspoken thoughts after the solicitor stopped speaking, and they hurt my head. I felt rather than heard a hiss emanate from Miss Taplow, and Evangeline's hand clenched mine so hard I thought it would break. When I looked at the row of servants I noted a small smile on the cook's face and a pout on the housemaid's. But Hillbeam stood with tears running down a face full of wonder, and fourteen-year-old Tessie appeared about to explode with happiness.

Despite my earlier certainty, despite the waiting cases at Hazelgrove, the sense of unease returned. I shook it out of my head. No. It was still nothing to do with us.

CHAPTER 6
Connie

I expected Katherine to be quick — but not *so* quick. It could not have been more than an hour and a half after she and Evangeline had set out when the doorbell rang. I expected to hear chatter, perhaps excited voices; but instead there were only a few murmurs until James's mother came to the hall. Then I heard a 'Good gracious!', followed by the unmistakable sound of sobbing. 'There, there, dear, the excitement has made you overwrought,' said Mrs King, and I imagined her leading Evangeline to her room, fussing over her, ordering beef tea or gruel, and insisting she lie quietly. Poor Evangeline.

Katherine's footsteps pattered down the corridor a few moments later. She opened the door, whisked through it, and closed it behind her as if she wasn't supposed to be there.

'What happened?' I whispered.

Katherine, eyes wide, advanced with a finger to her lips,

and whispered in my ear. 'Miss Quinton left almost everything to Evangeline.'

I gaped. 'Really?' I mouthed.

Katherine nodded. 'I'll tell you more on the way to Lion House. I asked Hillbeam for a short interview and she agreed. We can walk there.'

I drew back and studied Katherine. Her breath was coming rather quickly, and her face was a little flushed. 'Are you sure that's wise?'

'Oh, do stop it,' said Katherine, 'I'm not an invalid.' Her voice rang through the quiet room. 'Now look what you made me do!' she muttered, scowling. 'It's a good thing Mama will be busy with Evangeline. Come on, do.'

***

Katherine began the walk to Lion House determined to make a point of outpacing me, but as she told the story the speed of her narrative demanded she slow down, until we were ambling along the path as if we had nothing better to do.

'How did people react?' I asked.

Katherine glanced around, though we had not left the grounds of Hazelgrove yet and not a soul was about. 'Miss Taplow was the worst. She actually hissed. I don't think she meant to, but she couldn't stop herself. I felt Evangeline shrinking next to me. She got up as soon as she could. The solicitor asked her to remain so that they could discuss arrangements, but she just said, "Please write, or visit me at home," and practically bolted.'

'What about the others?'

'Hillbeam was very happy, as I imagine she would be

with forty pounds a year. The tweeny looked overjoyed, the cook seemed pleased, and the housemaid disgruntled, as if she had expected more.'

'But Miss Taplow was definitely angry?'

'Furious. She went over to the solicitor and actually asked when she would receive the money. "I would like to leave as soon as possible," she said, just as we were going. I don't know if she has family, or anywhere to go, but I think her nose was thoroughly put out of joint.'

We were at the perimeter of the estate now, and I drew the bolt on the wrought-iron side gate. 'Did Evangeline say anything on the way back?'

Katherine's mouth twisted a little. 'She kept saying "I never expected it," over and over again. I tried to reassure her that no-one would think badly of her, but I don't think she heard a word I said.' She waited while I closed the gate. 'I'm actually glad that Mama is making her rest.'

When we arrived at Lion House the door was answered by the housemaid. 'Come to see Hillbeam, I suppose? You'll have to wait your turn. Milady's in the parlour with the lawyer. Maybe she can spare you a moment or two.' She showed us into a cold, cheerless morning room, and a few minutes later Hillbeam came in.

'I'm so sorry to keep you waiting,' she said, sitting opposite us at the table. Already she looked a little less downtrodden. 'Would you like tea?'

'No, thank you,' I said, hastily, 'we won't keep you long.' The thought of Hillbeam ordering tea, and the scene which might ensue, would do no-one any good.

'What a day it has been,' said Hillbeam. 'I feel as if I

should be surprised at nothing.' Her slightly watery eyes rested on me. Was I imagining that speculative gleam?

'Miss Hillbeam…' said Katherine. 'It is Miss, isn't it?'

'Oh yes,' said Hillbeam, with a sad smile. 'Never been wed.'

Katherine smiled back at her. 'Miss Hillbeam, my colleague and I have a client in London, a Mr Hillbeam, who is looking for his family.'

'It is an unusual name,' said Hillbeam, eagerly, then checked herself. 'Your client… Is he — comfortable?' Her tone was wary.

I had to hide a grin. Poor Hillbeam, elevated in one afternoon from a lowly parlourmaid to a possible prey for fortune-hunters. 'I believe so. Please could you tell us a little about your family? Your brothers and sisters, in particular.'

Hillbeam considered. 'Well, there aren't many of us left, and only four of us got past an infant to start with. Jeremiah, the eldest, who died of a quinsy when I was ten, then me, then Ruth, then Jimmy, the youngest. He was apprenticed to a farrier over in Hazelmere, and he's the farrier there now. He never married, neither.'

'Could you tell us about your sister, Ruth?' asked Katherine. 'Is she still living?'

A spasm contorted Hillbeam's face. 'I wish I could tell you,' she said. 'I don't know myself.'

'Did you lose touch?' I prompted, gently.

'She ran away,' said Hillbeam. 'We were in service together here, and one day I woke up and she wasn't in the bed with me. I thought she'd got up early to get a start on the dusting, but we never heard a thing from her again. I was eighteen, I remember.' She said it without bitterness, as if any feeling had been worn away long since.

'Can you recall how old your sister was when she — left?' asked Katherine.

'A year younger than me — no, not even that,' said Hillbeam. 'Mother used to joke that Ruth hopped into her belly as soon as I popped out. Like a cat looking for a warm seat, she said.'

'Indeed,' I said. 'Would you mind if we passed on your details to our client?'

Her brow creased, then smoothed. 'As long as he's comfortable,' she said, 'I don't see why not.'

'In that case,' I said, 'I think our business is concluded.' I opened my handbag. 'Please could you let us know when your address changes?' I handed her a *Caster & Fleet* business card.

Hillbeam turned the thick pasteboard over and over in her large, worn hands. 'I will, ma'am,' she said, her face brightening. 'I certainly will.'

***

We almost upset the housemaid as we left the morning room. She coughed, glared at us, and moved down the hall to let us out. The door closed behind us with a sharp clack, and the crape bow on the knocker quivered.

Katherine and I fell into step. 'What now?' she asked.

'The evening train to London,' I said firmly.

Her pace slowed. 'Really?'

'Yes, really.' I took her arm. 'Miss Quinton's death has been declared to be from natural causes, and we have found not one, but two family members for Mr Hillbeam. We can continue the search for Ruth Hillbeam much better in London.'

'I suppose…' said Katherine.

'Are you worried about Evangeline?' I asked.

Katherine nodded. 'I'm not sure if she's strong enough to cope with this.'

'She may surprise you,' I said. 'Anyway, she has her parents and Norah, and you can write every day. I'm sure James will help too, once he knows.'

'Yes,' said Katherine, smiling. 'It will be lovely to see James.'

'I'm sure it will,' I replied.

Her smile broadened. 'Aren't you looking forward to going home?'

I sighed. 'I had a letter from Albert this morning,' I said. 'Veronica is still there, and apparently Mrs Jones threatened to give notice the other day.'

'Oh.' Katherine considered. 'Is that good or bad?'

I grimaced. 'I can't face hiring another cook. From what he said about Bee's behaviour, I'm a little worried that I might have to hire a nanny too.'

Katherine's eyes widened. 'What did she do?'

'She pulled the tablecloth off the table while they were having tea in the nursery. Luckily most of the plates are enamel, but still… Oh, and she popped George into the coal scuttle when Lily's back was turned. Apparently it took Lily a whole hour to clean him up.'

Katherine giggled. 'I'm sure you were never so naughty, Connie.'

I considered. 'I don't think I was. It's probably all from Albert's side of the family. Although he wasn't particularly amused.' I could see the lights of Hazelgrove now. Oh, if only I could wish myself home, without the noise and dirt of a train journey. 'Perhaps Evangeline could come and stay with you if she wants a change of scene. I'd offer too, but I don't think our house is particularly restful at present.'

'Perhaps,' said Katherine, absently.

I unbolted the gate and waved her through. 'We're not home yet, you know,' I said. 'We'll have to hurry if we're catching the next train.' I scrutinised her. 'Is your sixth sense quivering again?'

Katherine shook her head, then marched down the path to the house with renewed vigour. 'I don't know,' she said, her words floating back to me on the cooling air. 'Call me silly if you like, but I have a distinct feeling that we haven't finished here yet.'

I closed the gate and followed in Katherine's wake. Perhaps she was silly; but I had a distinct feeling that she was right.

Chapter 7
Katherine

As Margaret poured tea in the drawing room at Mulberry Avenue we heard three sharp taps above our head followed by the clanging of a small handbell.

'Father is driving me utterly to distraction,' said Margaret, slamming the teapot down with such force the cups rattled. Before either of us could rise, Ada stomped up the hall and then the stairs. Margaret shoved a cup at me.

'He has been quite ill,' I pointed out.

'And *hasn't* he enjoyed it. Thank goodness for medical school. If I were stuck indoors with him all day…'

Realising that as a female she would never be allowed to graduate, no matter how well she did, Margaret had left Oxford in the summer and started training at the London School of Medicine for Women.

'It's a chance to develop your bedside manner.' I listened to the murmurs overhead and wondered what

Father was demanding this time. Perhaps an obscure book from the disordered shelves of the study, or a glass of hot water with lemon. Margaret was right: he was enjoying every minute.

Margaret speared a crumpet and thrust it into the fire. 'I had my doubts anyway but now I'm certain I won't be suited for general practice. I shall go into research.'

My little sister was nearly twenty-one and quite lovely. Her hair — chestnut with a hint of auburn — was piled artfully in the latest style with a short curled fringe. Her deep blue eyes flashed under thick dark lashes. Wearing a fashionable suit in a shade of red I couldn't even hope to carry off, she looked unlike either a doctor or a scientist.

'What do you want to research?'

The ringing of Father's bell tinkled through the ceiling again.

'Untraceable poisons,' said Margaret with a wicked grin.

I chuckled. 'Well, to avoid your doing any research at home,' I declared, 'James will escort Father to Hazelgrove the day after tomorrow.'

Margaret's expression brightened. 'What a horrible thing to do to the Kings.'

'Don't be silly,' I said. 'It'll give them someone to fuss over rather than Evangeline. Meanwhile, you can come and stay with us.'

Margaret blinked. 'Oh.'

'I thought you'd want to.'

'Um, yes, of course. Although now that everyone else has moved out it would be nice to have the house to myself for a bit. I *could* manage quite well on my own here with the servants.' There was something distinctly shifty about the way she concentrated on scorching the crumpet. It reminded me a little uncomfortably of the half-truths I'd once given Aunt Alice.

I sipped my tea and feigned nonchalance. 'Yes, why not. There will always be Ada waiting on the other side of the door at midnight if for any reason she thinks you're gallivanting.'

Margaret met my eyes at last. 'You might be right. I suppose I'd be nearer to medical school if I'm in Bayswater and needn't rush home every evening. And if you're out on a case and James is busy at the press…'

'Mmm.' I said.

'So what *is* your latest case?' she asked, easing the crumpet onto a plate and slathering it in butter.

'We've just finished one and are considering our latest correspondence.' I refilled my cup and took a second scone. 'We've nothing terribly exciting at the moment, although Evangeline has requested we find out a little about the property in Primrose Hill. Obviously the lawyers are contacting the sitting tenant formally; we're just taking a look. No-one, apart from Miss Quinton's solicitor, had any idea she owned property other than Lion House.'

'Lucky old Evangeline,' said Margaret. 'I wish someone would leave me two houses and a heap of cash.'

'Well they won't, so keep your nose to the grindstone.' I took a bite of scone and pondered.

'What's the matter?' Margaret put her head on one side as she contemplated me.

'There's butter on your lip.'

'There are crumbs on your bosom, now that you've finally got one. But that's not what the matter is.'

I sighed. 'James has spent two days trying to find out if there is the remotest possibility of having a telephone put in at Hazelgrove. We're both very worried.'

'One would have thought she'd be thrilled to be an heiress.'

'I'm not so sure. I don't think anyone ever expected Evangeline to have to manage so much money on her own. Everyone is giving her advice, and she has to find new servants for Lion House if she's to let it out.'

'Can't she just live there?'

'Oh Margaret, don't be so silly. She's never been alone in her entire life.'

'Moss could lease it from her.'

I narrowed my eyes at her. I had said nothing of my suspicions to anyone but James. 'What's Moss got to do with anything?'

'He was here the other day. He was after a book about land management while visiting Father. Moss seems *very* fond of Hazelgrove.'

'Really?'

'Mmm,' said Margaret, and flashed another wicked grin. 'I'm considering giving up medicine and joining Caster and Fleet as a detective. What do you think? Oh, and Father's been receiving scented correspondence in purple ink. Usually he asks me to deal with his letters, but not these. Is it my daughterly duty to steam them open?'

'Behave yourself,' I admonished. 'They'll be full of the

usual nonsense from some maiden lady who believes in fairies and wants him to prove it. He probably can't face your withering sarcasm.'

***

Connie and I pored over a map in a small coffee-shop off Regent's Park Road.

'You really are worried about Evangeline, aren't you?' she said, watching me re-check the address for the fourth time. 'I've never known you so woolly-headed. Although it might be the baby of course. I've also never known you order steak for lunch.'

'The doctor says it's good for expectant mothers,' I said, folding up the map. 'It was steak or spinach.'

'A few months ago you'd have preferred spinach.'

'It's not in season and I can't bear canned,' I pointed out. 'But yes, I am worried.'

'She will be fine with some good advice. Moss could help, I'm sure.'

I looked sideways at her.

'You're not the only one to have noticed,' she said.

'Albert can mention it if he wishes,' I said. 'I certainly won't. It's not really advice she's lacking though, it's knowing where to start. She wants to let the house but all the servants are leaving.'

'Of course, Hillbeam is retiring.' Connie pondered. 'Will the annuity be enough to rent a place and live?'

'She's gone to live with her brother.'

'And if Jonah *is* their nephew, in all probability neither of them need worry ever again. What's happened to Tessie?'

'She's going back to school,' I said. 'Her parents are unsupportive but at least they can't complain about loss of income. Mrs Booth told Evangeline the countryside got on her nerves and she's going to Reading. Sukey is in a bit of a sulk. She hasn't decided whether to marry or get another post, but refuses point blank to stay at Lion House.'

'Goodness,' said Connie. 'I do sympathise. I've had staff for three years and I still find it a headache. Poor Evangeline isn't used to dealing with that sort of thing at all. How is she feeling?'

'Overwrought. Besides, she was actually rather upset by Miss Quinton's death even though she hid it well.'

'Try not to worry,' said Connie. 'It will work out. I'll see if Albert can drop some hints to Moss.'

It was only a short distance to Wright Terrace. The house and its tiny front garden were identical to its neighbours: a modern brick building with neo-classical mouldings round the door and windows. The door itself was recessed within a small porch and we could make out two bell-presses, though there remained one letter-box. There were bay windows top and bottom, both obscured with lace curtains, and the lower one made further private by virtue of a threatening object, presumably an aspidistra, lurking behind the lace on the inner sill. The road was quiet. Most of the delivery boys had long been through, although a telegram boy racing past on a bicycle nearly collided with a cab coming the other way. The subsequent bad language clashed with the neat hedges and polished doorknobs.

'Scuse me, ladies.' The postman stepped round us

towards the gate, shuffling letters in his hand. 'Was you after anyone in particular?'

'Not yet,' I said. 'I had heard that there might be a flat for rent. My sister is looking for somewhere and I wished to make sure it was suitable for a lady.'

The postman eyed us both in surprise, clearly trying to work out if I, a small redhead, and tall brunette Connie could be related. I let him wonder, it was much more fun.

He scratched his head under his cap. 'Could be. I never know till the names on the letters change, but there's three houses turned into flats along here. This one for example.' He nodded at number forty-two. 'And number eighteen and number thirteen — unlucky for some, ha! But no, you needn't worry. It's very respectable. Up and coming, this area, I reckon. Up and coming.'

'This seems nice,' said Connie, indicating number twenty-four. 'Quiet, and so close to Belsize Park.'

The postman shrugged. 'They're all nice. Though I can't say I'd be sorry if 42A moves on. Lots of letters. It's doing my back in, I tell yer. Good luck, anyway.' He stepped through the gate, whistling, and deposited a handful of post through the letterbox.

At the office Connie and I exchanged notes. There wasn't much to add to what we already knew. She had managed to catch a glimpse of a name while the postman was talking to me. *A Latimer Esq, 42a Wright Terrace.* But in terms of the area, it seemed Evangeline's investment was a good one. There was no sign of overcrowding and everything was very proper. As the postman had said, up and coming.

I typed up my report to send to Evangeline and handwrote a friendly note to add to it.

Connie was staring out of the window and I realised that in my concern over Evangeline and doubts about Margaret, I'd forgotten to ask after Veronica. Sisters were quite exhausting.

As I was sealing the letter the door to our office burst open.

James stood there, waving a piece of paper. 'I've had a telegram. Evangeline has shut herself in her room and now Mama is afraid she'll have a fit.'

Connie turned to him, aghast. 'I thought it wasn't certain that she'd ever had one.'

'It isn't and I'm sure she hasn't, but I'm not surprised she's shut herself in her room.'

'Why?' I went over to put my arm round him. He was trembling.

'Miss Taplow has instructed someone to challenge the will.'

'Oh no ... But —'

'That isn't all.' James's expression was grim. 'Dr Stokes still insists there's evidence of malice. He's managed to identify something he found in Miss Quinton's throat when he examined her. At first he thought it was a morsel of food — but it's a tiny piece of lavender.'

CHAPTER 8
Connie

As I took in what James was saying, my heart sank to the bottom of my boots.

Now we had no choice. Katherine and I would have to go back and get involved. And I simply *couldn't*.

I hadn't told Katherine, but I had arrived home from Hazelgrove to find utter chaos. I had had to wait on the doorstep for some minutes before my ring at the door was answered, and when Johnson finally admitted me he looked as if he had seen a ghost. Upstairs, from the direction of the nursery, I could hear voices which sounded like Lily and — could that be Albert? Surely the children were in bed?

'What is going on, Johnson?' I asked.

'You — you weren't expected, ma'am,' was all he could stammer.

'I can see that,' I said, removing my hat. 'Should I go up to the nursery, or is that a bad idea?'

At that moment I glimpsed a rounded form whisking out of sight down the hall. 'Who's there?' I called, and started in pursuit.

I was fully into the servants' hall before I caught up with Mrs Jones, who was, ominously, wearing her good coat and carrying a small case. 'Stop!' I cried, as officially as I could, and she froze as if I were the police. For a moment I felt gratified before realising that I was only delaying the fateful moment. 'Sit down and explain yourself,' I said, indicating a place at the table and taking a seat opposite.

'God-forgive-me-ma'am-but-it's-Miss-Veronica,' said Mrs Jones, as if reciting a Bible verse she had got by heart. 'Nothing pleases her. Since you've been from home I've had to plan all the meals, and she hasn't liked any of 'em. So I've had to cook two separate meals every mealtime, an' I'm worn to the bone, an' —'

'That will stop immediately,' I said. 'If she doesn't like your food she can have bread and cheese. Is there anything else?'

Mrs Jones, looking stricken, shook her head.

'Good. Please go and unpack.'

'She keeps coming into the kitchen *wanting* things,' she wailed. 'Just some toast at eleven, or crumpets with afternoon tea, or a mug of cocoa before bed.'

I sighed. '*Please* unpack, Mrs Jones, and I shall speak to my sister. After which I would like supper, if you don't mind.'

Mrs Jones shook her head violently, then changed her mind and nodded instead.

'Is there anything else I should know?'

'Nanny Kincaid's sister's been taken ill and she's gone to Scotland,' gabbled Mrs Jones. 'The master didn't want to worry you.'

'Ah.' That explained the uproar from above. 'I shall go to the nursery first, then.' As I left the room, out of the corner of my eye I saw Mrs Jones slump in her chair. *When I catch up with you, Veronica...*

Upstairs I found Albert pacing the nursery with a yelling George in his arms, rubbing his back, while a tearful Lily looked on. 'I don't know what it is, sir,' she said. 'He sleeps so well usually. I was just folding linen and he started awake all of a sudden.'

'How long has this been going on?' I asked.

Lily thought. 'Since Nanny Kincaid left for Glasgow,' she said. 'It's as if he knows she's gone.' A dreamy smile spread across her face for a moment before a particularly loud bellow from George chased it away.

'Hmm. Hullo darling,' I said to Albert, meeting him at his turning point and kissing his cheek, which I noticed was perhaps a little rougher than usual at this time of day.

'I'm so glad you're home,' he said, making to hand George over.

'One moment,' I said, whipping round in time to see a blue eye close hastily. 'Aha! I thought so.' I pulled down Bee's covers to reveal a wooden stick thrust next to the wall. 'I assume you've been poking your brother to wake him up.'

Bee, eyes screwed tight shut, shook her head as violently as Mrs Jones had done.

'Where did you get this, Bee?'

Bee was silent. I picked the stick up and handed it to Lily, who examined it. 'I think she's pulled it off her hobby horse, ma'am.'

'Ingenious,' I commented. 'No treats for you for the rest of the week, Bee, and you can say sorry to everyone in the morning. For shame!'

Bee's eyes were still tight shut, but her bottom lip stuck right out. I put the covers back over her, took George from Albert, and motioned to him to follow me.

In the boudoir I handed my coat to Violet, directed her to fetch my things and unpack them in the bedroom, and set about feeding George, who settled comparatively quickly to the task. 'You should have told me in your letter,' I said, trying not to sound reproachful.

Albert sat on the floor opposite me and sighed. 'Maybe. But you were busy.'

'Not too busy to come home,' I replied, stroking George's flaxen fluff. 'When did Nanny Kincaid leave?'

'Yesterday. A telegram came saying that her sister was gravely ill. Nanny is her only family, so of course I packed her off.'

'Good.' I glanced at the door. 'Is there any sign of Veronica leaving?'

Albert snorted. 'I doubt it. She's made herself too comfortable.'

'That stops at once. I've directed Mrs Jones to carry on as normal.' A thought struck me. 'Has my mother written? Or telegraphed?'

Albert shook his head. 'Not a line.'

'Oh dear.' George was already nodding off. I got up,

cradling him, and returned to the nursery, passing him carefully to Lily. Then I leaned over Bee's cot-bed. 'And *no more shenanigans* from you, young lady,' I muttered, to a sharp intake of breath.

There. Now I just had my sister to deal with.

***

I found the other cause of the trouble sprawled on one of the drawing-room sofas, reading a novel with a half-empty box of chocolates next to her. 'Have you any idea how difficult cooks are to come by?' I asked, swiping her novel — *Vanity Fair*, indeed — and putting it face-down on the table.

Veronica grimaced. 'She isn't very willing, is she?'

'You wouldn't try that sort of thing at home, and Mother has more staff than I do. My house, my rules.'

'Listen to you,' said Veronica. 'Do you know who you sound like?'

I resisted the urge to put my hands on my hips and square up to her. 'If our style of living doesn't suit you, Veronica, you can always go home.'

'You know I can't,' Veronica said shortly.

'Why, what have you done?' Veronica reached for her book but I picked it up and held it behind my back.

'It's what *she's* done!' cried Veronica. 'Although as it turns out...' She gave me a smug look and took another chocolate from the box.

'I hope you haven't eaten all of those today,' I said, eyeing the gaps in the layer. 'You'll make yourself sick.'

'I'm fortifying myself against Mrs Jones's cooking,' Veronica retorted.

'You'll need to,' I said, putting the lid on the box. 'I've told Mrs Jones that she is not to cook any separate meals for you, and you are not to ask her for any extras. If you want anything, you ask through Nancy. You are *not* to go to the kitchen.'

'Have you finished?' Veronica snapped.

I considered. 'For now, yes. Though I'd still like to know what's brought you here.' I sighed. 'You can stay so long as you don't turn the household upside down.'

A little smile wavered on Veronica's face. 'Thanks, Connie.' She eyed the novel in my hand and I passed it back.

I tracked Albert down to the study, where he was comparing two sheets of figures. 'Burning the midnight oil?'

'Hardly. Just checking something.' He shuffled the sheets together and put them in his top drawer.

'You don't have to stop because I'm here.'

'I know.' But he didn't retrieve them.

'You don't like violet creams, do you?'

Albert made a face. 'They're one of the few foods I won't eat. Disgusting perfumed things. Don't tell me you've developed a taste for them.'

'Don't be silly, I dislike them as much as you do.' I paused. 'Veronica was eating a box of them.'

'She would,' said Albert, with a look of distaste.

'No, but — they can't be ours, if neither of us like them.'

'Maybe she bought them,' said Albert.

'I doubt it,' I said. 'It was a large box. The sort of box

someone might give to impress you. I wonder —'

'Another mystery?' Albert smiled.

'Perhaps.'

Albert ran his hands through his hair, disarranging it slightly. 'I haven't asked you how you got on at Hazelgrove.'

'It was — interesting,' I said. 'I think we can let it rest for now.'

***

But as it had turned out, we couldn't.

Lavender in Miss Quinton's throat.

A challenge to the will.

Evangeline at risk of — I wasn't sure what, but —

'I don't know what to do,' I said. 'Well, I do, but — I don't see how I can.'

'You don't have to go to Berkshire,' said Katherine. 'You can stay here and manage the London part of the investigation. I could go back —'

'On the train, on your own, and investigate a potential murder?' retorted James. 'I don't think so.'

Katherine's eyes flashed green. 'Are you going to try and stop me?'

James sighed. 'Are you determined to go, Katherine?'

Katherine raised her eyebrows. 'Would you expect me to stay, with your sister in danger?'

James went to her and clasped her waist. 'Then I'll come with you.' He kissed her forehead. 'I'll wire Lord Marchmont and Nathan, and my editor at the *Chronicle*. It isn't as if they can't reach me at Hazelgrove.' He grinned. 'Maybe this is how I shall persuade my father to get a telephone installed.' One more kiss, and he was gone.

'I suppose that settles it,' I said. 'You and James look after Berkshire, and I'll get on with things here.' It was the perfect solution, and yet I felt as flat as a bottle of ginger beer that had been left open all afternoon.

'We could,' Katherine said, tentatively. 'Although I'd rather manage on my own if you're not with me —' She sighed. 'It's not ideal, but I can't think of another way. Can you?'

'It makes perfect sense and I really don't mind!' I cried, plastering a smile on my face as I went to take her hands. 'I'll look out the London files. You'd better go home and pack. Again.'

But I did mind. Nothing could be done about it, yet I felt very lonely as I sorted through the papers and sat at my desk. I read each document more than once; but rather than building up a picture of the case or a plan of action, all I could see was James and Katherine dashing about, finding clues and talking the case over in the library at Hazelgrove, while I fed George and scolded Bee and placated the servants at home.

CHAPTER 9
Katherine

'I am much recovered,' wheezed Father. 'And I'm delighted you were able to organise a magic lantern talk in the parish rooms this evening at such short notice. I'm sure it'll cheer everyone up. If my voice gives out, I'm sure James can stand in while Katherine operates the machinery. I suspect she knows it better but it takes a man's voice to carry, don't you think?'

The Kings sat mesmerised. James muttered something I hoped I'd misheard. Margaret was having lunch with Evangeline in her room, although I suspected that was less out of altruism than fury.

What with collecting Father and Margaret, and Father's insistence on bringing the magic lantern so he could 'entertain' his hosts, we weren't able to catch a train before eight-thirty, and didn't arrive at Hazelgrove until eleven. By that time, regardless of my impatience, I had to concede that James was right and we would have to wait till after lunch before descending on Lion House. But then he wouldn't let me go alone.

Everyone was annoyed with me. Connie for involving us on a case that was out of the city, James for being stuck with Father's unending stories, and Margaret, who still didn't quite believe that her professor had suggested she come and study a neurology patient in situ. She was right to doubt it, of course; I had suggested it to the professor rather than leave my sister alone in London. I had considered suggesting she stay with Connie and help with either Bee or Veronica, but since I actually wished to retain Connie's affection, not to mention sanity, decided against it.

So it was two p.m. before James and I took the trap and left Hazelgrove. Frost still lay thick in the shadowed lea of hedges and leafless trees. It would have charmed me if I hadn't been so agitated. James had insisted not only on coming with me but driving; whether because Mama had suggested it or because he was fussing, I couldn't determine. I missed Connie's common sense and felt concerned that she had some worry she couldn't share with me. Altogether, I felt thoroughly disagreeable.

'Shouldn't you be with Evangeline?' I snapped, itching to take the reins from him and hurry Blossom.

'Perhaps I'd like to see you at work.'

'You've seen me at work. You've even helped me in my work. But right now you ought to be with your sister.'

'Please don't tell me what to do, Katherine.'

I gritted my teeth and glared sideways. It was aggravating how handsome I still found him even when infuriated. I could think of a hundred things to say, but forced myself not to say them. The truth was we were both worried, and when that was the case we either both brooded or argued. It should have been Connie with me, only she was caught up with nursery chaos. Apart from anything else her trust in me made me brave even when I was scared, whereas James's fussing just increased my fear. Would motherhood really be this distracting? I smoothed my stomach and agreed with my child that he or she would be much better disciplined.

'Would you like to live here?' asked James.

It was so far removed from anything I was thinking that I gawped.

'Well, would you?' he said.

I stared round at the rolling slopes and pretty copses, the smoke streaming from the village chimneys into a clear sky. I drew in a breath of clean, fresh air tinged with woodsmoke and old leaves. Grubby sheep in a muddy field lifted their heads as if waiting for my answer.

'No,' I said. 'All this space makes me twitchy. I feel like things are peering at me from behind vegetation.'

'They do that in London.'

'Aspidistras don't count as vegetation. They're virtually human.'

It occurred to me that I ought to ask him how he felt but I was too annoyed. And I was jealous of Connie who, even if she had to drag the children and Lily and Veronica with her, could nevertheless make the London investigations where there were pavements, smooth roads and most importantly plenty of tea-shops. We pulled up outside Lion

House without any more being said.

Evangeline had told me that Sukey, with a little persuasion and a slight increase in wages, had agreed to stay on alone in the house during the day until she decided her future or a replacement was found. All she had to do was light fires to ward off damp and dust, but since I felt some sympathy for her wandering the house alone, I rather dreaded how she'd greet us. I was surprised when the door opened on our first ring of the bell. Even more surprised to find a man in a bowler on the other side. He doffed his hat to me, replaced it and appraised us both, as Sukey looked on with impatience.

'And you are…?' he asked.

'We could ask the same question,' said James.

'He's a copper,' said Sukey. 'And they're the Kingses. Are you all checking up on me? Cos I ain't done nothing.'

'Mr and Mrs James King,' said James.

'Relations of . . . Miss King, heiress?'

I could feel James bristling. 'Anyway.' The man put out his hand. 'Inspector Havelock.'

'Good name for a copper, ain't it?' said Sukey. 'Can you all come in and shut the door? It's like an ice-house in this hall at the best of times.'

'Good afternoon,' said James. 'Can you explain why you're here?'

'Of course,' said the inspector, stepping back. He waited until Sukey had scurried to the kitchen and we entered the drawing room. A fire composed of a handful of twigs warmed a space two feet in front of the hearth, and we huddled before it.

'I'm just having a look-see,' he continued. 'I gather you've heard what the good doctor has re-asserted, else you,' he addressed me directly, 'wouldn't be here. I imagine you've been instructed by Miss King.'

I opened my mouth to reply but James was quicker. 'We —'

'Funny,' said the inspector, scanning him from head to foot with a grin, 'I always thought Miss Fleet was more feminine and wore prettier hats.' He winked at me. 'There's a lot of respect for your agency, Mrs King, or should I say Miss Caster. A lot of respect. Even this far out of London. Word travels. Now there's no official investigation yet, but as you'll have guessed, it's coming. The inquest is being reopened tomorrow and then the chief constable has to decide how to proceed. No exhumation requested, thank heaven. I've been sent up from Reading to see how the land lies. Not long got here. Took a while to track down young Sukey in this mausoleum. Found her with her feet up in the kitchen eating cake and reading the illustrated papers. Can't blame her I suppose, it's lovely and toasty in there, but I hope Miss King isn't paying her over the odds.'

'Strictly —' I began.

'Strictly I shouldn't be in here without your sister-in-law's permission,' completed the inspector. He tapped his nose. 'Bad housemaids are a policeman's angels in disguise. Anyhow, as it happens, I'm glad you're here. It means we can look round together and neither one of us can accuse the other of interference. How's that?'

I prodded James with my foot. With a small sigh, he put

my hand through his arm and patted it; however annoyed we were with each other, we both knew when to watch and listen. 'Yes of course, inspector.'

'Let's start in here, shall we?'

Room by room we toured the house, beginning with the cold drawing room, a morning room only marginally warmer by virtue of size, the dining room and a positively glacial study. Not one fire was big enough or hot enough to toast as much as a crumb. I wondered if I should ship Ada down to chivvy Sukey, but suspected it would make her leave all the sooner. There was wallpaper everywhere bar the panelled study. Old designs from half a century ago in the main; exotic birds in every colour adorned the walls of the morning room, bright in corners and faded where the sun must fall on them. The tapestry on the chairs matched in reds and blues.

In the drawing room swans flexed their wings among arsenic-green reeds on a black background, and gazed down on velvet-covered chairs and fine inlaid cabinets. Antiquities abounded as well as bowls of dried blooms, glass jars with wax roses and stuffed squirrels, and a glass-topped table displaying mourning brooches and miniatures. Landscapes, portraits and architectural sketches covered the walls, women with flowing hair stood before backdrops of lavender fields under hot suns, and figures in Grecian dress stood dwarfed by dry ruins.

The upper rooms, including the maids', were mostly shrouded in dust cloths which revealed nothing. Miss Quinton's own room was pleasant if old-fashioned, the four-poster bed piled high with heavy silken counterpanes, and velvet curtains in imperial purple were tied back with golden cord.

'She died here of course,' said Inspector Havelock. 'No sign of any suffering, apparently, but the doctor couldn't swear to it. Nothing to suggest anything untoward. Now let's play fair, Mrs King. We've both been observing throughout the house. What do you see?'

I looked round once more while I considered my answer. I wanted to think about what I'd seen for myself before sharing my thoughts. I certainly didn't want the inspector either misinterpreting my ideas, dismissing them, or taking them for his own. The bare essence of them would suffice, and he could make of them what he would.

'A rich lady's bedroom,' I said. 'A well-thumbed book, a carafe for water…' I picked up the book. It was about Australia. Turning the pages, I saw fine watercolour illustrations and small text. Father would love it.

'Mmm,' said the Inspector, opening the drawers in a small desk and making a tour of an adjoining room complete with hip bath and commode. 'Where do you suppose she kept her personal papers?' This time he looked at James.

'The solicitor has most of them,' he said. 'My sister has Miss Quinton's journals.'

'Is that all?'

'As far as I know.' James shrugged.

We made our way downstairs and stood in the freezing hallway. Discordant singing came from behind the baize door.

'Shall we…?' I suggested, indicating the kitchen.

'Nothing down there but cake,' said the inspector. 'I came in that way, remember, courtesy of young Sukey. If you want a bit of a warm-up before you drive home, why not? But me, I'll go out the front door like a gent. I've got a train to catch.'

'We could drive you there,' said James. I stood on his foot but he ignored me. 'It's not so far out of our way.'

'Thank you, no,' said the inspector. 'I'll probably warm up better walking to the station.' He tipped his hat and made his way out.

James made to follow him.

'No,' I said. 'We haven't checked the kitchen.'

'You heard what he said —'

'Well, I still want to look,' I said, pushing the baize. 'You can stay here or you can come, or if you're in two minds, perhaps you could inspect the butler's pantry. There's a few rare bottles of port in there according to the inventory. You might want to reassure Evangeline.'

'Oh very well.'

The pantry, along with the larder, was just inside the servants' quarters, on the north side of the house. James stepped within, lighting the candle on its ledge, and slammed the door shut.

Rolling my eyes, I made my way to the kitchen. It was indeed warm. Sukey had discarded the paper and was waiting for the kettle to boil while selecting a piece of shortbread from a tin. She jumped at my approach.

'Ooh you didn't half scare me ma'am.'

'I'm sorry.'

'I heard a bang and was sure you'd gone out.'

'That was Mr King slamming the pantry door.'

'Ooh he don't want to do that ma'am. It sticks something awful.' She offered me the biscuit barrel and made the tea.

'I'm sure he'll be fine,' I said, glancing into the frosty kitchen garden. 'It could be worse, he could be stuck in the privy.'

She giggled. 'Miss Q didn't like men. She wouldn't have minded if he was.'

I sat at the table and accepted a cup of mahogany tea. 'You're getting married, aren't you?'

'Yes, though I'd hoped for a bigger nest-egg from her, truth be told. My intended is opening a shop. Still, I shouldn't have expected more. She never did approve of her maids giving in to their passions.' She giggled but didn't, I noticed, blush.

'It's kind of you to stay on and work so hard,' I said. 'Miss King is very appreciative.'

Sukey shrugged. 'She's a nice lady. And it's a bit more for my bottom drawer, ain't it?'

'Aren't you nervous all alone?'

'Nah, I can manage.'

'What do you think of Inspector Havelock coming?'

'Huh,' said Sukey. 'What's a policeman? Who's he think he is? Miss Q must be turning in her grave, all these men tramping about the place. The doctor, the lawyer, Mister fancy-hat Havelock, that bloke from London, even Mr King, begging your pardon.'

A muffled thump came from the passageway.

'What "bloke from London"? Did he come in?'

'Nah,' she said. 'He just wanted some letters.'

'What letters?'

'I didn't know, did I? I said they'd all been taken by the lawyer. But the bloke said he worked for the lawyer and something had been left behind. Well, it seemed likely. It was all of a fuss wasn't it, after she died. Hillbeam was in that much of a dither. I told him there weren't nothing. How was I meant to know?'

'Know what?'

'That she'd shoved them away in a drawer. Mind, she was a bit strange sometimes. Age, I suppose.'

'What was the "bloke" like?'

Sukey grinned. 'Well he was foreign like I said, but he had lovely dark eyes with long lashes. If I wasn't engaged…'

A louder thump came from the passageway. 'Have you still got the letters?' I asked, opening my bag.

'Maybe,' said Sukey cheerfully, with a pointed look at my purse.

Chapter 10
Connie

If I had hoped my return would restore Bee's behaviour to normal, I would have been gravely disappointed. Every time I visited the nursery Lily had a new offence to report — flicking porridge at her brother, refusing to put on her shoes for a walk, and once, memorably, having to be captured and returned by the park-keeper after running off while Lily was attending to George.

'I wonder if it's because Nanny isn't here,' I said, half to myself.

'She'd never *dare* if Nanny was here,' said Lily. 'It might just be her age.'

I gaped at her. 'Is this — usual?'

Lily considered. 'It isn't *un*usual.'

'Does it go on for a long time?' I ventured.

Lily smiled, and underneath it I could see how tired she was. 'I think some children stay that way.'

A brief letter from Nanny Kincaid had arrived that

morning. Her sister had had an operation, seemed to be recovering well, and Nanny would start for London as soon as her sister was out of danger. I could have kissed her large, firm writing. 'Hopefully you won't have to manage too much longer, Lily,' I said, showing her the letter. 'I would take the children this afternoon but I have a business call to make, and I don't think Miss Bee would behave any better in a lawyer's office than she does in the nursery.'

Lily looked horror-struck. 'Oh ma'am, what an idea!' She glanced at Bee, who was sitting on the ottoman kicking her heels, and who gave her a sweet smile in return. I wouldn't have trusted her an inch.

Despite Nanny's good news, I went to my boudoir to dress for the call with a heavy heart. If Albert had been at home I could have poured it all out to him, and we probably would have laughed over it. But Albert had been out at meetings since breakfast, and would not return until five o'clock at the earliest. He had mentioned it lightly enough; but it was unusual for him to be 'booked up' to such an extent, and I resolved to ask him how things were at the very next opportunity. With a vague sense that I was, somehow, addressing whatever problems there were, I pinned my hat firmly in place, pulled on my gloves, and picked up my *'Miss Fleet'* briefcase.

The offices of Miller, Parkinson and Strutt were on the top floor of a ramshackle building in Lincoln's Inn Fields, and were reached by a staircase which grew less grand with every landing. Mr Strutt's office however was rather pleasant, with a view over the square which, while currently damp and leafless, would be bustling with life in a few months' time. Mr Strutt himself, though, was as dry as a winter leaf and not at all representative of his name, sidling behind the desk as though he was about to burgle it.

'Do take a seat, Mrs, er —'

'Miss Fleet,' I said, taking the chair before the desk. 'That is my business name. I am a partner in the Caster and Fleet Agency.'

Mr Strutt scrutinised me for a few seconds before replying. 'Mm,' he said. 'And you are acting for…?'

'I understand that Miss Taplow is contesting Miss Quinton's will,' I said firmly.

'Ah. Yes.' Mr Strutt opened his desk drawer and took out a folder, removing a letter packed with slanting, looped handwriting in blue ink. 'We received this from Miss Taplow, in which she states her intentions.' He looked up at me. 'You did not answer my question, Miss Fleet.'

'If Miss Taplow is contesting the will then I am acting for the main beneficiary, Miss Evangeline King.'

Mr Strutt did not blink.

'Would I be able to see a copy of Miss Quinton's will?'

The solicitor's mouth twitched and he reopened the folder, drawing out a long envelope on which was written, in a black-letter hand, *Last Will and Testament*.

'The will has been read, and I believe your partner was there. So —' He pulled a sheet of thick cream-coloured paper from the envelope and opened it on the blotter.

'*January 2nd, 1894*,' I read. 'So this was a new will?'

Mr Strutt nodded. 'I received a note from Miss Quinton when I came into the office after the Christmas holiday, asking me to come to Lion House at my earliest convenience. It was dated 25th December.'

'Christmas Day…' I mused. What could have caused Miss Quinton to issue such a command, on such a day? 'Is this will very different from the previous one?'

The solicitor regarded me for some time before answering. 'I regard a client's last will and testament as confidential until it is read.'

'Do you think Miss Taplow has reason to contest the will?'

A slow blink. 'It is my belief that Miss Quinton had given Miss Taplow to understand that she would receive a considerably more substantial legacy than the extant will provides for.'

That sounded like a *yes*. 'Have any other legacies in the will changed substantially?'

I met his eyes, and he looked down at the paper. 'Hillbeam's bequest was originally a straightforward sum of money, of lesser value, as was' — his finger ran over the page — 'the tweeny's. Otherwise it is much as before.'

I scrutinised the foot of the document. Miss Quinton's signature was a little shaky, but legible. Witnesses: Mr Strutt, and… I peered at the second signature, which was written in a flourishing yet hard-to-read hand, with a thick nib. 'Who was the second witness?'

'Ah, that would have been Mr Latimer. He was a house guest at the time, I believe.'

'The sitting tenant at Wright Terrace?'

Mr Strutt slid the will back towards him. 'That is correct.' He folded the document and put it into the envelope; the envelope into the folder; the folder into the drawer. I sensed the matter was being tidied away with the paperwork. 'Miss Fleet, if you have no further questions, I am a busy man.'

***

I took a cab to the office and found Reg rocking on his chair and tapping his teeth with a pen. He returned to the vertical hastily and squared up the papers on his desk.

'Keeping busy, I see,' I remarked, as I hung up my coat.

It had become apparent early in the life of the Caster and Fleet Agency that we would need both an office and someone to staff it. Reg, with his neat handwriting, ability to assume a reasonable accent, and all-round usefulness, was the obvious choice. He was used to our ways, loyal, brave — and I suspected he had a sneaking admiration for my nursemaid Lily. I hadn't had to play that particular card yet, but I held it in reserve.

'Sorry Miss F, you caught me at a quiet moment. It's been all go this morning. Shall I put the kettle on?'

'Please.' I sat at my desk and noted down the key points of my conversation with Mr Strutt. 'Have you typed and sent the letter to Mr Hillbeam?'

'I have, Miss F, and posted it at midday.'

'Marvellous. Have you managed to find out anything about Mr Latimer at Wright Terrace?' I tried to keep my voice neutral, but Reg, who was leaning on a filing cabinet with his hands in his pockets and watching the kettle boil, turned so precipitately that he nearly overbalanced.

'What's to do, Miss F?' he said, when he had recovered himself.

I sighed. There was no point in priding myself on my ability to keep a secret when I was so obviously an open book to Reg. 'Don't get too excited. I just learnt some new information which means that Mr Latimer might be a bit more important than we thought.'

'You've come from the solicitor, haven't you? Is it about the will?'

Luckily the kettle sang out at that moment, and Reg's ensuing bustle with a tea-cloth, cups and the milk which we kept on the windowsill gave me time to compose a reply. 'In a secondary manner. And that is absolutely confidential.'

'Yes Miss F,' said Reg, saluting as he delivered a china cup of strong tea.

'Thank you.' I sat at my desk and composed a wire to Katherine: *Latimer witnessed will STOP Please read Miss Q's journals for mention of him also ask servants if or when he visited STOP C.* 'Can you send this to K — Miss Caster when you've finished your tea, Reg. And step up your enquiries about Mr Latimer. I want to know where he goes and what he does. Put a watch outside the house, if you can.'

'Right Miss F.' Reg drained his cup in a way that made me wince for his throat, put on his cap, took the slip of paper, and went off whistling.

I sat back in my chair and sipped my tea. What else could I do at this point of the day?

My answer came through the double knock of the telegraph boy. I went down the stairs, congratulating myself on how much less rickety they were than Mr

Strutt's, and received the envelope.

How funny, we must have crossed each other, was my first thought on seeing the familiar *Caster* and *Hazelgrove*. But my mirth ended there.

E ill STOP Received anonymous letter STOP Sending you for analysis STOP Await letter at Marylebone K

How long would it take a letter to reach me from Berkshire? My brain tried to compute the distance and the steps required, and gave up. Could it arrive today? I wasn't sure.

What was in the letter, and why was Katherine sending it to me?

I shook my head to clear out the questions, wrote a brief and hopefully cryptic note for Reg, and clattered downstairs.

***

A letter, addressed in a flurried version of Katherine's hand, arrived in the first post the next morning. I had spent an abstracted evening when I returned from the office the day before; but Albert was quiet too, and had retreated to the study after dinner. I was almost glad; I didn't want to worry him about a letter which I didn't even know the contents of.

'See,' remarked Veronica, waving her fork at the letter. 'Katherine can address her letters any way she likes, and no one gives a damn about it.'

'Veronica!' I exclaimed.

She grinned. 'I didn't mean to shock you, Connie!'

'Do be quiet,' I said, and got up. 'Excuse me, I need to look at this alone.'

As I went upstairs to my boudoir I distinctly heard Veronica exclaim 'How rude!' *Just you wait, Veronica*, I thought. *When I have a spare minute, I shall deal with you.*

I sat at my bureau and opened the envelope, scared to catch my breath. Inside was a single sheet of paper and another envelope — a plain white one, with *Miss King* and Hazelgrove's address written on it in shaky capitals.

Katherine's note said: *You'll see why I've asked you to analyse the enclosed. Perhaps if we can find out where it all came from, it will give a clue to the sender. Poor E is prostrate and the doctor is with her. K*

Frowning, I picked up the second envelope.

It didn't take me long to catch Katherine's meaning. The note within was not written but composed from letters cut from newspapers, in a mix of upper and lower case. It was short and to the point.

I KnoW yOu Did IT

CHAPTER 11
Katherine

Sukey looked surprised when I offered to come with her to retrieve the letters.

'Oh, stay here. You should be resting. I knows where everything is.' She gazed at my stomach with such innocent concern I decided a thorough check against Miss Quinton's inventory couldn't come soon enough.

'It's no trouble,' I said, rising. 'Besides, we have to rescue Mr King.'

James was just inside the pantry with a guttering candle in one hand and a bottle of port in the other. Before he could speak I brushed a cobweb from his shoulder and raised my eyebrows. His lips twitched.

After a great deal of rummaging in a sideboard which she ought to have known well, Sukey opened a small leather box. 'Oh fancy. Here they are in with the apostle spoons, not the fish knives. I must have thought of St Peter and got muddled.'

'I'm sure you did,' I said, taking three letters from her.

'They're only plate too,' she added.

'Sorry?'

'The apostle spoons.'

'I expect the fish knives are silver.'

She looked nonchalant as she took my shilling. 'Couldn't say, ma'am.'

Outside, James helped me into the trap and handed me the reins in silence. We were well out of the gate before we both started laughing.

'I'm sorry,' I said, 'but you were being so very husbandy.'

He shrugged, putting his arm around me and gently laying his other hand on my stomach. 'It wasn't that much of a punishment. I found the port delicious.'

'I thought Miss Quinton didn't approve of strong drink.'

'You misunderstand. According to Mama, Miss Quinton didn't approve of *other* people enjoying *hers*. She often poured herself a large glass of sherry while everyone else was served lemonade. Anyway, what will you do with those letters? Steam them open or hand them to the solicitor?'

'Neither until I've spoken with Connie,' I said. 'She and I are in this together.'

***

We returned to Hazelgrove for afternoon tea and then Standish drove James, me, Father and the equipment down to the village to set up for the magic lantern talk.

It took place at six p.m. and went very well. Father's voice held out, fortified with honey and lemon mixture in a jar which — judging from the whispers I heard — half the audience thought was brandy. I had the feeling that no-one, not even the villagers who attended the fire-and-brimstone chapel, had ever heard anything so thrilling or so full of unlikely beasts. But Evangeline had been right not to come. I felt rather than saw the stares as James and I entered the hall to set up, and a few mutterings when the show was over. Yet someone was pleased to see me.

'Oh Mrs King, that was wonderful!'

It was Tessie, her servant's uniform replaced by a neat plain costume. 'Would your father come and talk to the school?'

'I'm sure he would.'

'I'm teaching the little ones like I used to,' she said with delight. 'All thanks to Miss Quinton. My parents...' Her face dropped a little. 'They'd have rather I stayed in service, but I hated it.' She cheered up again. 'I thought I'd get sacked at Christmas when Miss Quinton found me reading in the study, but after that she took an interest in me. Everyone thought she was harsh, but I think she just didn't like people wasting their skills. I want to be a credit to her.'

'I'm sure you will be.'

Tessie smiled, then spotted my handbag. 'That's so pretty. It makes me think of the little embroidered herb-filled pillows Miss Quinton had all round her bed. She was a terrible sleeper, forever trying a new concoction. The day she died we just thought she'd finally found a mixture to help her get off. I felt so awful when Hillbeam found her and she'd passed on. Surely it's a misunderstanding, what they're saying now. Old people have to die eventually, don't they?' She paused, her bright young face solemn for a moment and then cheerful. 'They were so pretty though. The pillows, I mean. Would you mind . . . would you ask Miss King if I could borrow one and copy the pattern?'

'I'm sure you can,' I said, wondering where they'd been stored. 'I don't suppose you have Mrs Booth's forwarding address in Reading, do you?'

'Oh, she said Reading was too provincial,' said Tessie. 'So she went to London to sign up with the Monsarrat Agency. They specialise in fancy cooks, you know. It was nice to meet you again, Mrs King.'

It had been such a lovely evening. On the journey back to Hazelgrove, with Father asleep in the carriage, James held my hand and kissed me just as he used to. I felt the baby's kick more distinctly, as if it were dancing. The moonlight shone across the frosty fields, and a tiny part of me wished we could travel for ever and never worry about anything.

I was right to wish it. When we arrived everything was in uproar. Margaret was waiting for me in the hall, her usual calm replaced by anxious pacing. I could hear Evangeline sobbing before we'd even removed our coats.

'Oh dear,' said Father. 'Do you think she's upset to have missed the talk?'

'No!' Margaret and I said together as James bounded up the stairs.

'Go to the drawing room, Father,' I said. 'It's been a busy evening. I'm sure dinner will happen eventually.'

'Well, if you're sure, but I'll pop into the library first.'

He ambled off.

Margaret dragged me into the morning room and thrust something into my hand. 'You have to go back to London. You and Connie must sort this out once and for all. This utter filth didn't come from here. The postmark is Charing Cross.'

My mouth fell open as I read the cruel words printed on a piece of card.

'That could be a ruse. Someone could have...'

'Popped up to London to post a letter and popped back again? Not everyone is as rich as you are nowadays, Katherine.' She saw my face. 'I'm sorry, I didn't mean that the way it sounded. But Evangeline has been crying so hard I fear she will finally give herself a fit after all. This isn't the actual letter, it's a copy.'

'You haven't left the original with Evangeline?'

'Of course not! I've sent it to Connie to puzzle out. Listen to her. The doctor is considering a sedative —'

'Dr Stokes?'

'No, Dr Stokes has gout and is saving himself for the new inquest. It's his junior partner, Forester. Seems a decent sort, all things considered. Quite young.' Her eyes glazed a moment. 'It was him or no-one. Of course we didn't show him the letter, just said she was distressed by the scandal-mongering. Her mother has tried smelling salts and now her father is suggesting laudanum.'

'No!'

'Quite. I promised Evangeline you'd solve it all. She said she'd calm down if you spoke with her. Oh and I hope you don't mind, I sent Connie a telegram.'

'Good.'

'In your name.'

'Oh. Well —'

'And I wrote a letter in as close to your handwriting as I could manage, to put in with this tripe.' She waved the card.

'Why —'

'Because I had to catch the last post, and I thought she'd pay more attention if it came from you. She'll never notice. You have a terrible scrawl when you're panicking.'

'I never panic.'

I rolled my shoulders. I felt utterly exhausted all of a sudden and the agitated squirming in my stomach didn't help. The thought of another train journey didn't appeal, but there was nothing else to be done. 'We'll go back tomorrow, as you said.'

'What, me?' Margaret glanced towards the ceiling. Evangeline's sobbing had calmed. 'Yes we shall, if you insist. That awful thing came from London, I'm telling you.' She chewed her lip. 'Perhaps I should have kept it for James to look at. Oh blow, I forgot, a telegram came for you.' She took it from her pocket and handed it to me. 'Of course, I could stay here and research the case with Dr Forester.'

'I thought you might be missing someone in London.'

'Why would you think that?'

I raised my eyebrows at her, then gasped as I read Connie's message. *Latimer witnessed will STOP Please read Miss Q's journals for mention of him also ask servants if or when he visited STOP C.*

If only I'd known before I'd visited Lion House or spoken to Tessie. But then I thought: *if this is distressing me, what on earth will the telegram Margaret sent be doing to Connie?*

***

I reassured Evangeline that Connie and I were doing all we could, and reassured Mama that having dinner would be a good thing for everyone.

Evangeline's eyes kept turning to the journals. Just seeing them seemed to make her nervous.

'I think I'll take those,' I said. 'I'm sure they're full of derogatory comments about men which I intend to learn by heart.'

Evangeline gave me a wan smile and managed to succumb to sleep in the end without sedatives, but with the aid of Father reading *Alice in Wonderland*. No-one was entirely sure if it was simply to stop him talking that she finally dozed off. I fell asleep between the fish course and the entrée. Despite my protestations James carried me to bed, where I fell into a deep slumber.

I woke in the middle of the night. Somehow I knew I was the only one in the house awake except the mice scurrying in the walls. When I peered onto the landing I saw no lamplight under any door.

I climbed out of bed and, wrapped in an eiderdown, took Miss Quinton's journals to the chair by the dwindling fire, lighting a candle from its embers to read by. James snorted as he turned over in his sleep, and my baby seemed to jump before also settling back into slumber.

'Shh, now,' I whispered.

There were six thick volumes. Miss Quinton's sparse entries began when she'd been a little over twenty, and continued until two weeks ago. Her spiky old-fashioned writing was hard to read, but in truth she had managed to make travels on the continent even during periods of immense turmoil sound dull. Most of the entries recorded things like: *Weather too hot and locals smile too readily. The food is greasy and abounds in tomatoes.* I despaired of finding anything of interest.

My head starting to ache, I picked up the last volume, flicked through and the blurring words suddenly formed into a possible reference to Mr Latimer. It was June 1891. *A insists somewhere near Belsize Park or Primrose Hill is more suitable. He says he would prefer to come to Reading. I say why? It is nowadays quite hideous and bordering on the industrial. He knows that is not why I would prefer him to remain at a remove. He seems content, but I am not sure I trust him. After all, he has his father's eyes.*

Chapter 12
Connie

A light tap on the boudoir door made me jump. 'Come in,' I called, attempting to put the newspapers surrounding me into some sort of order.

'Sorry to interrupt, Connie, I came to see how you were —' Albert broke off and stared at me.

'Fine. I'm fine,' I said wearily, reaching to pin up a strand of hair which had somehow managed to come loose and which I had been pushing out of the way for the last half-hour. I was aware that I must present an odd picture, kneeling in the middle of a sea of newsprint armed with a pair of scissors, but I was sure it wasn't my strangest incarnation.

'Good.' Albert took a step back. 'I won't disturb you then.'

'You've already disturbed me,' I said, perhaps a bit more testily than he deserved. 'What is it?'

'I was going to ask if you wanted to come and say hullo

to Moss when he arrives, but —'

'Yes, of course. A break would do me good.' I scrambled to my feet. 'I'll come down —'

'You might like to wash first.'

The twinkle in his eye made me turn to the dressing table. 'Oh no...' I clapped my hands to my face, then realised they were the source of the trouble. My eyes were surrounded by inky smears, and somehow I had put a crooked black smudge under my nose.

Five minutes later I was considerably cleaner (though the same could not be said of the towel), and I was on my way downstairs as the doorbell rang. Johnson scurried by and bowed Moss in.

'Good morning, Moss,' I said.

'Ah, good morning, Connie,' said Moss, unbuttoning his coat. 'Albert in?'

'Yes, he's in the study. I'll go and —'

'Don't worry, I'll find it.' Moss handed his coat and hat to Johnson and strode down the corridor, leaving me standing on the third step.

'Nice to see you too,' I remarked, once the study door had closed, and went back upstairs, shutting the door of my own room rather loudly behind me.

So far I had identified two papers from which most of the letters had come, cut from headlines and sub-headings: the *London Evening Standard* and the *London Daily News*. The capital *K* and *W* were the only two letters I had not managed to find. I had rejected the *Times, Telegraph, Graphic* and *Sporting Life*. I sighed and picked up an *Illustrated London News*, and the *W* jumped out at me almost immediately. A matching *K* was on page 29.

I sighed, gathered the rest of the papers into a bundle, picked up the letter and the magnifying glass I had been peering through, and got to my feet. The first part of the puzzle was solved: the letter had been created from London papers, and with its Charing Cross postmark, had definitely come from London. But that was only the beginning.

I sat at the bureau and scrutinised the letter again. The letters had been cut out with short-bladed scissors, since the biggest had needed two snips to cut out their length. Violet's workbox was in the corner, left there with a small heap of stockings to darn, and I rummaged for her embroidery scissors. Yes, just the right length. The letters were evenly cut, with space round each, and had been pasted on the paper in straight lines, with no smears of glue to spoil the effect. Whoever had done this had taken their time. I shuddered at the thought of the unknown person, the tip of their tongue sticking out as they positioned each letter carefully on the page.

Her tongue. Embroidery scissors.

Unless the sender was a man practising an elaborate deception. I sighed.

The paper was of reasonable quality — not flimsy but not thick, and probably purchased from a high-street stationer. The envelope was a ready-gummed one. This person would not use a seal. And they read the *Standard* and the *Daily News*, not the *Times* and *Telegraph*.

Someone comfortable, but not well-off.

I trained my magnifying glass on the shaky name and

address. All were written in capitals, and the odd slant of the letters, with a smudge or two, suggested that they had been written with the left hand. The even flow of the ink must mean a fountain pen.

Someone who writes letters often enough to own a fountain pen...

...and whose writing Evangeline might recognise?

I gasped. Evangeline's circle of acquaintance was not large; she could not know more than, what, twenty people outside her immediate family?

But why? Why do such a thing?

I pushed the letter away, took a blank sheet, and uncapped my own pen.

- *They might really believe E did it.*

I almost put a line through it then and there. Evangeline wouldn't hurt a fly.

- *They want to frighten E — but why?*
    - *To make her stay at home? But she rarely goes out.*
    - *She might give up the inheritance? What would happen to it?*
    - *To make her ill — perhaps to*

I couldn't write any more. I turned the paper over and went downstairs in search of distraction. Surely I was just being morbid... But I could see the words I *hadn't* written very clearly in my mind's eye.

My plan to join Albert and Moss evaporated when I heard raised voices coming from the study. Johnson was nowhere to be seen. *How odd*, I thought. *I don't think I've ever heard them disagree before.* For one thing, Moss was too phlegmatic an individual to muster up much in the way of anger. I paused, more from curiosity than an actual desire to eavesdrop:

'I'm not investing any money in that scheme, Moss, and I strongly suggest that you don't either.'

'Have you considered that you're being over-cautious, Albert?'

'I don't think one can be too cautious when looking at an investment scheme that's come out of nowhere, and frankly, is promising the earth.'

A pause. 'I must admit that I had expected a better return.' Moss sounded peevish.

'The market goes down as well as up, Moss.'

A chair scraped. I did not linger to hear more, but crept back upstairs. I considered visiting the nursery, but I was in no mood for another instalment of *The Misadventures of Bee*. So I tidied myself, put the letter in my bag, and hailed a cab, giving the office address. If Reg were there he could tell me any news; and if not, perhaps a period of quiet reflection might do me good. If nothing else, I could at least get some fresh air after being shut up with newspapers for half the morning.

But as the cab rolled along I found myself thinking of Moss. It was so unlike him to be cross — and over money? From the little that my husband had said on the matter, as he was reticent about discussing money, Moss's small private income had grown considerably since he had entrusted it to Albert. And it was understood that Moss would inherit the bulk of their father's estate in due course.

He must want money now, I thought. *But why?*

The answer came quickly. *To marry Evangeline...*

Bile rose in my throat. *He doesn't know about the letter*, I told myself. It isn't his fault that this business with Miss Quinton has happened, and Evangeline has inherited —

London papers...

Handwriting Evangeline would know —

I covered my eyes with my hands. *He wouldn't. It doesn't make sense.*

If he proposed she'd jump at the chance to leave this mess behind her —

I opened the window for fresh air as the cab began to slow. 'You all right, ma'am?' asked the cabbie. 'You look a bit peaky.'

I couldn't answer. I put the money into his hand and turned away.

***

The office was empty, as I had suspected it would be. Given the choice of book-and-paper research or an opportunity to hang around in the street, possibly with friends he had scared up for the purpose, Reg would always choose the latter. Then again, it had proved useful on more than one occasion.

Once I had gone through the post and found nothing urgent, I found the map Katherine and I had consulted the other day and measured the distance between Wright Terrace and Charing Cross with my finger and thumb. It must be at least three miles, and no tube line connected the two places. Yet three miles was a cab ride, or an hour's walk for a fit man. Three miles was nothing.

And Mr Latimer, we had heard, received many letters. So presumably he would possess a fountain pen —

I*f only Katherine were here*, I thought, getting up to light the gas stove and set the kettle going. She had the other parts of the puzzle — Miss Quinton's journals, the run of Lion House, and access to Evangeline — while I was stuck in London building theories out of thin air.

The creaky step, halfway up the second flight of stairs, did its job. Someone was coming. I thought about taking the kettle off the stove, then left it in case it was Katherine. Or Reg. Either was much better than being alone with my thoughts.

A knock. It must be a client. 'Come in!' I called, folding the map.

'*Here* you are,' said my older sister Jemima, looking aggrieved. 'I'm not a detective, you know. I called at your house and no-one knew where you were. I had to work it out.'

'Congratulations,' I said. 'What have you done with Joseph?'

'The same as you,' said Jemima. 'Nanny has him.' She sat opposite me. 'Are you going to make tea, or what? One lump, please.'

As I made the tea I reflected on the strange circumstance where getting away from the house had led to me waiting on Jemima. 'Why are you here?' I asked, putting a cup in front of her.

'You don't sound very pleased to see me,' said Jemima, peering into the cup. 'I hope this is China tea. Is the water safe to drink in this neighbourhood?'

'*Yes*.' She took a cautious sip and made a face. 'Have you come about Veronica?'

'Heavens no. Why would I care what Veronica does? Not that I would know. Do you have any biscuits?'

'This can't be a social call, or you'd never have bothered to come here.' I looked more closely at my sister. 'Jemima, what is it?'

'I'm glad I found you,' said Jemima, putting her cup down hastily, so that it rattled in the saucer. 'I need help, Connie, and you're the obvious person to ask. I want you to shadow Charles.' Her tone was as thin and sharp as a stiletto blade. 'I think he's having an affair.'

CHAPTER 13
Katherine

I arrived at Simpson's at twelve-thirty on Saturday. 'Anyone in need of a lunch partner?' I said.

'About time too.' Connie embraced me warmly. 'I've been picnicking with Reg for what feels like days. It's really not the same, although I've learnt to do tricks with a bandalore. You never teach me anything so useful. I've ordered chops for both of us. Let's talk of nothing but frivolity for a while. It'll be better for your digestion.'

As it turned out we were both hungry enough to make conversation, frivolous or otherwise, superfluous until we had satisfied ourselves. 'I'm so glad to be back,' I said, as I put my knife and fork on my empty plate. 'And now...' Looking at her more closely, I saw shadows under her eyes. 'What is it? Is it Bee? Or is it Veronica? Margaret's asked her to go out for afternoon tea. Or is it...?'

'Don't worry, I'll explain later,' said Connie. 'It's nothing to do with Miss Quinton. Tell me what you discovered.'

I lifted my embroidered handbag into my lap. Something nagged at my memory.

'What's wrong?' said Connie.

'Not sure,' I answered. 'Anyway, the second inquest yesterday was reported in this morning's *Times*. An open verdict. Even the jury thought the fleck of lavender was simply inhaled in her last moments. It's a very dried-flower sort of house. Oh bother, now I've remembered. I'll have to ask James to enquire about the pillows and he won't have the least idea what I'm talking about.'

'Pillows?'

'Tessie says Mrs Quinton had embroidered herbal cushions in her bedroom, but I don't recall seeing them.' We decided against dessert but ordered coffee.

As we drank it, I showed her the letters Sukey had given me. 'I asked Hillbeam about these yesterday. She was rather shamefaced and said she'd hidden them from Miss Quinton in the fish-knife box because the handwriting made her upset. I fear for the whereabouts of the fish-knives. Fortunately Sukey's eye to the main chance doesn't stretch to the potential of letters.'

'Don't keep me waiting any longer — what do they say?'

I spread the envelopes out on the table. 'What's the first thing that strikes you?'

Connie peered a bit closer. 'The postmarks are London but the writing — it's a continental script.'

'Anything else?'

She frowned and shook her head.

'Look at the contents.' One was a letter from *The Monsarrat Agency for Quality Kitchen Staff,* asking for a reference for Mrs Booth and offering a replacement. It was dated three weeks before Miss Quinton's death.

'So that means she was already intending to leave.'

'Yes. There's a note in the journals about it. It seemed quite amicable.'

'Why would Hillbeam hide letters from an agency?'

'She didn't. She hid *one* letter from them by accident. The other two are from someone else entirely.'

'But —'

'It's not the same handwriting, it's just similar. One person's writing looks much like another's if they were taught the same way. Look at the letter Margaret sent in my name.'

Connie chuckled. 'It did look like your panicky handwriting.'

'I never panic.'

'Of course not. Presumably Hillbeam thought they were all from the same person. So it must be the others which she thought would upset Miss Quinton.'

I spread the letters for her to see. Each was a simple note, one dated in May, one in October.

Henrietta, said the first, *might I see the gift entrusted to you? I have not forgotten. Have you?* The second said *Henrietta, why are you so stubborn? I told you last year what would be the outcome if you persisted.* Each was signed with a tangle of initials that were impossible to decipher. LJ? TL? TJ? JZ?

'Sukey, when pressed, said the "bloke from London"

was "kind of foreign,"' I explained. 'When pressed, *foreign* meant he wasn't from the village. *I'm* kind of foreign to Sukey. I put on my best French accent and she said, "Oh yes, he sounded just like that." But when I tried another sentence in my best Cockney she said, "That's right" as if they were the same thing. It's hopeless. She did say he was from Mr Strutt, but Mr Strutt didn't mention it to you. When I asked Hillbeam she started shaking as if she anticipated imminent arrest, and she admitted similar letters came once or twice a year. Miss Quinton always became very angry and often burned them on receipt.'

We paid the bill and left. The doorman hailed a cab for us and, finding it harder than I'd anticipated climbing inside, I didn't pay attention to the destination. Settling against the cushions, I waited until I caught my breath before asking.

'Brompton,' said Connie. 'Mr Latimer owns a small gallery-shop specialising in sculptures. I thought perhaps we might be potential customers. Were the journals of any use?'

Finding my notebook and still feeling rather dizzy, I gave my report.

'In general, Miss Quinton wrote daily when she was abroad and weekly when at home. Curiously, however, in...' I checked my notes, '1852, there are no entries after May, when she had not long returned from Florence. She simply writes: *I must place my souvenir safely. Perhaps Adeline...*'

'*Safely* is an odd word.'

'Presumably it's something precious. A painting,

perhaps?'

'Not another wretched painting. No, I'd say it's an ornament. *Safely* suggests fragility.'

I grinned. 'There are knick-knacks all over Lion House; you could be right. James is hoping to check through the inventory with Evangeline shortly. I hope anything valuable is locked away. Perhaps Mr Strutt knows of a safe-deposit box at the bank.'

'Was there anything else?'

'She and Mama's mother were close friends from childhood and subsequently she was interested in Mama even though her "*budding intellect is rotted by pandering to the desires of a man and constant production of children*". She did soften a little when...' I pressed my hand on my stomach as if to protect my baby from hearing, 'James's siblings died one after another.' I felt myself choke up, but regained my composure and continued. 'The first reference to Evangeline is at Christmas 1861. "*I should have spent this season somewhere warmer. I feel cold to my very heart. Hillbeam is attentive but so quiet. I wish for energy, for discussion. I would have Dorothea King here for company, but she has had another child and will not go anywhere without it. I could not bear to listen to its wailing. Or dear Adeline — but that is impossible.*"'

'Huh,' said Connie. 'I was more or less told not to visit some of my acquaintance if I brought the children.'

'What did you do?'

'Struck them from my acquaintance.'

'Very wise. I shall do the same.' I turned a page in my notebook. 'Evangeline is mentioned with increasing affection after the age of about ten. She cooled a little when Evangeline fell in love, but when that came to nothing Miss Quinton was furious about the talk of epilepsy, and championed Evangeline ever stronger. She very much wanted to teach her the sciences, but the Kings apparently would have none of it.'

'Sciences?'

'Miss Quinton had a passion for them. According to Tessie she annoyed Mrs Booth "something cruel" by forever making potions in the kitchen. The scullery was too cold and depressing for experiments, although not too cold and depressing for Tessie to spend half her time in.'

Connie pulled a sympathetic face; whether for Mrs Booth or Tessie I wasn't sure.

'Is there anything in there about poor Hillbeam?' she said. 'She ought to have been pensioned off years ago.'

'Only passing mentions,' I said. 'It seems she'd worked there so long, Miss Quinton thought of Hillbeam as part of the furniture and couldn't bear letting her go in case she'd be inconvenienced. There are vague complaints about Hillbeam's increasing slowness but they're countered with lack of enthusiasm for new blood. Not to mention wanting to retain her capital. I think she cared only for herself.'

Connie glanced out of the window. 'We're nearly in Brompton. What does she say about Mr Latimer?'

'Nothing, which in itself is odd.' I paused. 'But there are several brief references to a man called *A* from 1887 onwards. To begin with they're vague and a little bad-tempered. "*A has arrived. I had hoped he never would… Why need I worry about A? He is well set up…*" Then last year she says, "*I wonder as to A's motives… Needs must A will visit Lion House in October. It is discomforting… A says Taplow is nought but a snob. He is too smug. Men can be such arrogant fools.*"'

'It's hard to argue with that.' The cab had stopped. Connie half-opened the door and peered out. 'Wait here a moment.' She sprang across the pavement and returned with a downcast face. 'It closed at midday today. How annoying. Never mind, come home and I'll show you what I've found out about the anonymous letters.'

It was good to be back at Connie's house. Albert was not home, and Connie made no comment about it. Silence from upstairs suggested that order had been restored in the nursery, and finding out that the children had just been laid down for a nap, Connie asked if we could be informed when they woke. I felt like asking if I could join them instead.

Reg had sent a wire. *Gallery shut STOP Guess you'd go home STOP Am on his trail report later STOP.*

'At least someone's getting somewhere,' I said, pondering the newspapers and journals from which Connie had cut letters.

Connie began to pour out tea. 'Yes. I hope Veronica and Margaret —' A decisive ring at the doorbell interrupted her. Moments later the two of them burst in, giggling like schoolgirls. They both pulled up short at the sight of us.

'Where have you been?' Connie said, her eyes narrowed.

'We've been slumming it!' exclaimed Veronica, flinging her hat across the room. 'We were taken to the music hall! It was the most marvellous thing! Why have I never been before?'

'The music hall?' I said. 'Which one?'

'Taken?' gasped Connie. 'Who by?'

Margaret threw herself into a chair and helped herself to cake.

'The Merrymakers.' She looked straight at me with her head on one side. 'I understand it's quite respectable for ladies.'

'You needn't worry about who by,' said Veronica, smoothing her hair but not meeting her sister's eyes. 'We're grown women after all, and they are both gentlemen.'

'That's not the point,' snapped Connie. 'Come and speak with me in the morning room immediately.'

Alone with my sister, I forebore to explain to her that she was not yet twenty-one. Margaret looked unrepentant, yet I saw something in her face that suggested she was worried. I decided not to jump to conclusions.

'Whose idea was the Merrymakers?' I asked.

'Not mine,' she answered. 'Although it was fun. It's just that —'

'What? Did anything happen? Are you —'

'Don't fuss, Kitty. I need advice and you're all I've got.'

My mind raced and it took all my self-control to portray calm.

'It's nothing as bad as I can see you're imagining,' said Margaret. 'It's just delicate. There's this man —'

'What man? I knew there was a man! Who is he? What has he —'

'Kitty, calm down, it's not good for the baby.' Margaret

101

seemed to be collecting her thoughts. 'He works in the hospital laboratory. Today was very odd. He was as gushing as ever to start with, but on the way back, when I explained that I'd been visiting friends at a house called Hazelgrove, he went quiet and became rather cool towards me. I mean, I don't want him, but *who* does Mr Frank Taplow think he is?'

CHAPTER 14
Connie

'Just because *you've* forgotten how to have fun,' muttered Veronica, flouncing into the morning room and attempting to fling herself on an upright chair.

'I assure you that I haven't, Veronica,' I said, taking a seat opposite her. 'However, while you're staying here I am in charge of your safety. You can't just run off to a music hall with some man!'

'It wasn't some man!' cried Veronica.

'Who was it, then?'

She bit her lip. I had her.

'Was it the same man who sent you the chocolates?' I asked, gently.

Veronica nodded to the table.

'And you — like him?'

She snorted as if no-one but her had ever been in love before.

I spent a while pondering my next question. 'Does

Mother know?' I had been going to say *approve*, since in my experience Mother knew everything, generally before I did, but *know* seemed more neutral.

'Oh, Mother knows all right,' said Veronica bitterly, twisting her handkerchief till I feared she would rip the cambric.

Now it made sense. I could imagine the scene at my family home; Mother icy and imperturbable, laying down the law until Veronica stormed out. I remembered the many occasions when I had been subjected to one of Mother's tongue-lashings, or worse, silence, and felt a pang of sympathy. 'If you'll tell me who he is, and perhaps let me meet him, I could visit Mother and try to bring her round to the idea —'

Veronica stared at me in amazement, then burst out laughing. I stared back at her, and that made her worse. She slapped the table, chortling. I considered slapping her on the pretext of bringing her out of hysterics, but decided it would probably be wiser to wait her out. Eventually she subsided, and wiped her streaming eyes.

'What's so funny?' I asked.

Veronica took her time about answering, dabbing at her eyes with her handkerchief. 'The problem isn't that Mother doesn't approve of Richard,' she said, flatly. 'It's that she does.'

'Ah.' Now I understood.

'We met at a ball, a frightful stiff affair with dance cards and a swan carved out of ice and Mother breathing down my neck. I managed to sneak into the garden and saw a summerhouse which I thought would be a good hiding place. So I rushed in and Richard was there, reading a newspaper. "You look like Cinderella fleeing from the ball," he said, and we got talking.'

'I see.'

'We have so much in common,' said Veronica, her eyes shining. 'We both like dogs, and sunsets, and long walks —'

Long walks? I thought, remembering various occasions when my sister had flatly refused to move from her armchair, but kept the thought to myself and continued to listen.

'And when we went back to the ball Mother saw us, and she's been dropping hints and advising me and pushing me in his way ever since.' I hadn't realised it was possible to look smug and irritated at the same time, but Veronica managed it remarkably well.

'So what will you do about it?'

The smugness vanished from Veronica's face. 'What do you mean, do?'

'You heard me. I assume your — Richard's intentions are honourable —'

'Of course!' cried Veronica, and then a secret little smile flickered across her mouth.

'Hmm.' I regarded her sternly. 'He's proposed, hasn't he? And you've accepted.'

Veronica gawped at me. 'How did you know?' she whispered, putting a hand to her throat, where, I suspected, a ring was strung on a chain. Just as I had worn mine, secretly, before my engagement was public.

'You forget that I have some history in that department,'

I said, smoothly. 'So everything is actually fine. You love each other, and Mother approves. Time for you to go and pack.'

Veronica's mouth dropped open. 'But —'

'But nothing. You can't sneak off and get married just because Mother's a bit annoying.' I rang the bell to summon Violet. 'I'll come with you if you like, and talk to Mother, but if you're going to be married you'll have to learn to fight your own battles. And Veronica —'

'Yes?' Veronica looked as if she didn't know which end was uppermost.

I grinned. 'Congratulations.'

***

I sailed into the drawing room feeling rather pleased. At least I had sorted out one family problem, and Veronica would be off my hands shortly. I had done my best to push yesterday's conversation with Jemima to the back of my mind. Her worried face, her twisting hands, so like Veronica's and yet so different. I had said I would think the matter over. And I had not had that talk with Albert yet, either. *One thing at a time*, I had told myself.

But one thing was resolved, and that meant I would have to deal with either Jemima or Albert.

But not yet.

Katherine and Margaret were sitting together on the sofa, very sisterly and confidential. 'Should I come back later?' I asked.

Katherine looked up at me. 'Margaret knows a relation of Miss Taplow's,' she said.

'Oh.' I sat down in the nearest armchair, feeling limp.

'He isn't very exciting,' said Margaret. 'He thinks I'm wonderful.'

'That's nice,' I said. I wasn't sure I could manage two younger-sister conversations in a row.

'Apparently the Taplows have had a reversal of fortune,' said Katherine. 'Which might explain Miss Taplow's expectations from Miss Quinton's will.'

'I see.' My forehead felt tight, as if a headache was beginning. 'Where is Miss Taplow now? Didn't you say that she left as soon as the will was read?'

'We could write to Mr Strutt and ask,' said Katherine. 'But if she has family here...' She turned to Margaret. 'Could you ask your Mr Taplow?'

'He isn't *my* Mr Taplow,' said Margaret, huffily.

'Since you let him take you to the music hall, and we're conducting an investigation into a potential murder, I think he could be your Mr Taplow for that purpose.'

Margaret thought it over. 'If I'm helping with your investigation, do I get paid?'

'If you come back with information, possibly.'

Margaret brightened. 'I could pop into the laboratory on Monday and thank him for the outing, I suppose.' Her eyes gleamed.

'Good,' I said. 'Oh, and there was another young man I wanted to ask you about.' Margaret looked defensive, and suddenly I felt like a well-meaning but blundering maiden aunt. 'I mean Dr Forester,' I added hastily.

Margaret's expression didn't change. 'What about him?'

'Weren't you going to discuss Miss Quinton with him?'

'Oh yes.' Margaret assumed a businesslike air. 'He

undertook most of her care, whatever Dr Stokes says. Although she didn't have much time for doctors, not until she became properly ill.'

'Do you know what was wrong with her?' I asked.

'Oh, old-lady things,' said Margaret, vaguely. 'Well, not exactly, but her heart wasn't strong, she didn't sleep well, she complained of being tired, she was liverish. Dr Forester had prescribed her a digitalis preparation for her heart, but he didn't think she took it half the time. We had a really interesting conversation about patients and the psychology of being a doctor —'

'Could you write that down?' I asked, since Margaret appeared to be floating off into her own little pleasant world.

'Of course.' Margaret gave me a scornful look and pulled a little notebook and pencil out of her bag.

'Where could I read more about digitalis, please?' I asked, as humbly as I could.

'You could start in your library,' said Margaret. 'Tell you what, I'll go and see what I can dig up there for you.'

'That would be very kind,' I said. 'Shall I ask Nancy to bring you tea there? And perhaps cake?'

'Ooh yes please,' said Margaret, and for a moment she looked fifteen again.

I rang and gave my order to Nancy. 'And the same for us, please,' said Katherine.

'Oh, I'm not hungry,' I said. 'Besides, I'll probably have to escort Veronica home fairly soon.'

Katherine waited till Nancy had departed, then patted the sofa beside her. 'Veronica's a big girl,' she said.

'Tredwell will look after her.'

'It isn't that,' I said. 'It's — well, family stuff.' All the other 'family stuff' — Jemima, Moss, Albert and Bee — crowded in on me, and it was all I could do to stop myself holding up my hands to ward it off.

'Oh, Connie.' Katherine gave me a sympathetic look, and that was it.

'There are so many — *things*, all at once,' I managed, squeezing the words past the lump in my throat.

Katherine rubbed my back. 'Do you want to talk about it?'

I shook my head. 'I'm not even sure about half the things.' The ridiculousness of it struck me and I began to giggle, until a laugh turned into a sob. I covered my mouth in a panic. I couldn't cry, not now, not with Veronica and Margaret in the house, and in front of the servants —

'Digitalis,' mused Katherine. 'Isn't that from foxgloves?'

'Herbal pillows,' I choked out. 'Oh, *stupid* family getting in the way!' I cried, and smacked the nearest cushion, which fell on the floor and rocked gently for a second or two.

'It's what families do,' soothed Katherine.

I leaned down, picked up the cushion, and bashed its centre with the palm of my hand. 'At least that's one thing Miss Quinton didn't have to worry about.' I waited for Katherine to agree, but she didn't speak. She was staring at the cushion as if it might bite her.

'Unless she did,' she said softly. '*His father's eyes...*'

'Excuse me?'

Katherine shook herself, rather like a terrier. 'I could be

barking up the wrong tree entirely,' she said. 'We've managed with snippets, and minutes snatched here and there, and I may be making seven from two and two —'

'Maths was never my strong point,' I said, in a daze.

'But you're right about family,' said Katherine, putting her hand on mine. 'Whether or not Miss Quinton had family, she affected the lives of *several* families. She took an interest in the Kings, Hillbeam served her for years, she gave a home of a sort to Miss Taplow — and disappointed her. We need to sit down together with all the pieces of information that we have, and solve the puzzle.' She closed her eyes.

'Don't you drift off as well,' I said, 'I've had quite enough of that this afternoon already.'

Katherine's eyes snapped open. 'Sorry, Connie. I was trying to remember what Hazelgrove looks like in the summer. It's been a while.'

I frowned. 'Is now a good time for that?'

'Yes,' said Katherine, as Nancy came in with a tray. 'Yes, it is. Because when I closed my eyes and thought, I saw the village, and the road to Hazelgrove, and the meadows either side. And I remembered the foxgloves everywhere, waving in the breeze.'

Chapter 15
Katherine

We still had a case to close.

My heart lurched when I saw James enter the tea-room, just as it had four years ago when I first realised I'd fallen in love with him. The days we'd been apart seemed like weeks. Now here he was, somehow fresh despite the train journey, his eyes twinkling as he approached. Our embrace was as fond as it could be in public, and made two old ladies tut. The baby kicked, I giggled, and the old ladies tutted louder.

'I felt something,' he whispered. 'Was it…?'

I nodded and a look of wonder crossed his face before he turned to present Keziah Hillbeam and a stooped, red-faced man I vaguely recognised from the village, whom James introduced as Keziah's brother. Jimmy Hillbeam stood, solid and unemotional, as if formed directly from the soil of Berkshire, too sensible to allow excitement to cross his lined face.

Unlike James and her brother, Miss Hillbeam was neither fresh nor calm. Her eyes darted around as if she was trying to swallow London in one go. Her grey hair was taut under a frilled black hat. Her heavy grey worsted overcoat, faded from former finery, was old-fashioned and a little loose; but fresh trimmings showed here and there.

'Those are pretty buttons, Miss Hillbeam,' I said as the waitress brought our tea. 'I've never seen the like.'

She blushed. 'It's so strange to hear a lady call me "miss". I've been a parlourmaid for so long. But thank you kindly. They were our mother's,' she said. 'Dorset buttons. No-one makes them any more. They were all the thing once. I wanted to make this coat my own, you see. It was Miss Quinton's, you know — maids can't be choosy. Only with her passed before, it doesn't feel right somehow —' Her lip wobbled.

'Steady on, Kez,' said Jimmy Hillbeam.

'I wouldn't have worn it today,' Keziah continued, 'but it's the warmest one I've got. The wind goes right through me these days…'

'The buttons are such a pretty colour too,' I said. 'Like foxgloves — pink and purple. Or lupins perhaps. Or hellebore maybe. I've never seen the gardens of Lion House in the summer. It must look lovely when everything is in flower.'

Keziah and Jimmy eyed me as if I were mad.

'Well, ma'am,' said Jimmy, scratching his head. 'A garden's a garden. We let Mother Nature take her course. We don't go in for all this forcing things into square shapes like you got in London parks. In the summer we got hollyhocks as high as your hat, but no hellebore. It's called Christmas rose for a reason, ma'am. Beats me how anything grows in London when the sky's sorta yellow. Is that normal?'

I glanced outside to see if he was right, and saw Connie's familiar shape making for the door.

'He's here,' I said, as Connie entered, followed by Jonah Hillbeam.

Keziah, Jimmy and Jonah stared at each other for some time: the small, worn-down woman of sixty-six, her weathered brother and the confident wiry man in his mid-forties. Now they were close it was impossible not to trace the likeness in their noses and ears, the shape of their heads. Trembling, Miss Hillbeam said, 'Oh, you're the spit of Ruth . . . why didn't she tell me?'

And in a bound, Jonah caught her up out of her chair and hugged her as if his life depended on never letting her go. His hard eyes sparkled with tears, and when she pulled out of his hug she looked into them and said, 'Your pa must have been Jonas Simmonds... Oh the poor maid, the poor maid... Why didn't she tell me?'

'Is that the man who abandoned her?' He growled and clenched his fist.

'No!' she exclaimed. 'Not Jonas — you don't understand.'

Poor Miss Hillbeam, tears soaking into her gloves, told of a lad who'd died from lockjaw after cutting himself on a scythe, a lad she'd always thought her sister was in love with.

'There wasn't much time for courting, but they must

have managed it somehow. He'd have done right by your mother. And if only she'd told me, I've have gone with her to face Ma and Pa. There'd have been words, I don't doubt. But we'd have managed. It wouldn't be the first family in the village with a little'n not knowing his sister was really his ma, would it Jimmy? If only she'd come to me.' She wrung her hands and wept, appalling the ladies on the next table into leaving. 'She needn't have run away. It's not right what happened to her.'

'Don't you know where she went?' Jonah Hillbeam turned to us, his face also wet with tears as he reached for his aunt's hands to comfort her.

'We're still trying to find out,' said Connie.

'Take all the time you need,' he said. 'I don't care what it costs, neither. I got rich despite everything.'

'If only we'd known!' sobbed Keziah.

'You can't make it right,' said Jimmy in his slow voice. 'Best let the living take care of the living. Let's get acquainted, young man, and then we'll go along to the temperance hotel for the night. You can come back with us in the morning if you like. See where we grew up, and that.'

'You're not going to no hotel tonight,' declared Jonah. 'You're coming home with me. People know me as a hard man, but that's because life's made me tough. As soon as I married and held my first child, I knew I'd move heaven and earth to find my family. Now I've found it, I ain't letting it go.'

We left them in peace and, paying their bill, stepped into the street. A thickness in the air spoke of imminent fog. I hoped someone had warned Keziah and Jimmy. They had both been gasping a little already, and for a moment I imagined poor Ruth arriving in London with her secret kicking inside her, struggling to breathe.

'I still can't track her down,' said Connie, breaking into my thoughts. 'The workhouse recorded her leaving shortly after giving birth to find work, saying she'd be back to collect her baby. But she never did come back. And of the possible death records — where do I start? There are so many people and so many spellings. There's a Ruby Hilbeem, a Ruthe Hillbeam, a Ruth Hilbean and all recorded as dying soon after Jonah was born. None of them had a home address. One of them was found in an alley. In reality Ruth Hillbeam could be any of them or none of them. That's not even including all the desperate girls without surnames. In a way I feel Jimmy is right: let the living take care of the living. I — we have other things which are more urgent.'

'Mr Latimer, for example?' I said.

'Are you sure he didn't just supply Miss Quinton with art?' suggested James. 'You've seen Lion House, Katherine, it's bursting with classical pieces.' He turned to Connie. 'Evangeline and I went through the inventory. I think we know how the silverware has become "misplaced". Sukey didn't like "them old-fashioned paintings and lumps of stone". Some of the latter are ancient artefacts, but she called them "mouldy old things". Roman, Greek, a Phoenician glass goddess and so on. You can't believe how delicate they are and how old, and yet they've survived. A bit like Miss Quinton.'

'It doesn't strike me that she was delicate,' I pointed out.

'True. Poor old Jimmy — should have retired years ago, just like Keziah. Even at his age he does a bit of smithing and a bit of shoeing but Miss Quinton had hired him to check on the pony every day and prepare the trap when needed. I'm glad at least she gave Keziah a pension.'

'You could be right about Mr Latimer, but I still think I'll visit his shop,' said Connie. Despite having, as far as I could tell, resolved what I liked to think of as the Veronica conundrum, she was still a little distracted. 'Then we'll concentrate on the letters. When do you think Margaret will report back?'

'She's agreed to meet Frank Taplow this evening,' I said, my face heating at a conversation in which I'd offered to chaperone her and she'd reminded me of every time I'd climbed in at a window, worn boy's clothes or sneaked in at midnight.

'You two had better go home.' Connie smiled at us. 'I'm sure James is all smutty under that beard and needs sorting out.'

'Oh I very much am and I really do,' said James, and grinned.

Connie went pink. 'Could you hail us a cab each, Mr King,' she said with dignity. 'Some of us have work to do.'

***

Margaret sent a wire at nine p.m. *All well STOP Returned Mulberry Ave to leave you lovebirds alone STOP Check with Ada if you don't believe me STOP Report tomorrow STOP*

'How sweet,' said James. 'And it's Susan's night off too.

Whatever shall we do with ourselves?'

We lay curled in each other's arms on the sofa, my hair flowing over his shoulders, his hand gentle on my stomach as the baby danced.

'I'm glad to be home. Your father was driving me mad,' James confessed. 'Although I'm intrigued by the scented letters.'

'Oh goodness, has she managed to track him down at Hazelgrove?' I said. 'Even Father must have had enough by now. I'm so happy to have you home too. I can't get going without you.'

'You said you could manage perfectly well.'

'I can, but you're like a muse. Seeing your face every day, ridiculous as it is, makes my brain work.'

James laughed, then scratched his chin. 'I know it's the style but I'm thinking of shaving it off. Would you mind?'

'If you do and we have a girl, Albert will say that's why.'

'I don't care, do you?'

'Not in the slightest.'

He gently untangled himself from me and rose to go to the cabinet. 'Shall we have a night-cap?'

The baby lurched, making me feel dizzy and a little nauseous. 'I'll settle for cocoa. I'll go and make some.'

'As you wish.' James picked up the bottles one by one. 'Since when did we have two bottles of port?'

'Susan said one was sent to the agency this afternoon,' I said, stretching before making my way to the kitchen. 'Reg brought it while we were out at dinner. There's a label somewhere: *From a satisfied customer*. I hope Connie had one too. Although Albert probably has plenty. Is it a good vintage?'

'Very good,' said James. 'Your clients have excellent taste.'

It was cold in the kitchen. I hugged my shawl around me as I heated up the cocoa Susan had left. I loved our little home, and now that James was back, it was complete.

Cupping the mug in my hands, I returned to the warm sitting room expecting to find him on the sofa waiting for me.

And then I saw him on the floor, a deep red stain soaking into the rug.

CHAPTER 16
Connie

My eyes were closing over a novel when the telephone shrilled. I looked at my watch: half past nine. Surely only Katherine would telephone at that hour. I laid my book aside and padded into the hall, anticipating the servant's call.

But Johnson was speaking into the telephone himself. 'Yes, I'll make sure I deliver the message.'

'What message? To whom?'

He jumped. 'It's Mrs King, ma'am, but she can't —'

I seized the receiver. 'Katherine, what is it?'

'James has been poisoned,' said Katherine. 'I telephoned to warn you. If you've had a bottle of port from the office, don't open it. I must go.' And the line went dead.

***

I rushed into the study. 'Albert, I must go out. Someone's sent Katherine a bottle of poisoned port and

James has drunk some.'

'What?' Albert dropped the papers he was holding and got up. 'Is he all right?'

'I don't know.' Suddenly the world swam, and I felt Albert's arms supporting me.

'Steady, Connie.' He helped me to a chair. 'I'll ring for a cab.'

'It could have been us,' I said. 'It could have been *you*.'

'Don't worry about what ifs, Connie.' His tone was abrupt. 'Sorry. That didn't come out as I meant it to.'

'It's all right.' I got up, and my eye fell on the desk, which was littered with paper. 'What are you working on at this time of night?'

His face closed. 'Now isn't the time to discuss it.' He turned as the study door opened. 'Johnson, can you step outside and hold a cab for us? We're going to the Kings' house.'

***

Katherine answered the door herself. 'He's conscious, and Dr Farquhar's here.' She looked exhausted, and Albert took her arm as we went upstairs, more slowly than usual.

James was tucked up in bed, seeming rather embarrassed as Dr Farquhar took his pulse. 'Sorry, everyone,' he said, lifting a languid hand from the covers. 'I think I fainted. Perhaps it was a warning against shaving off my beard.'

I took a seat by the bed. 'If you were anyone else I'd think you were delirious, but you sound quite normal.'

He managed a feeble chuckle, and Katherine leaned down and kissed his forehead. 'That'll teach you to steal our port,' she said, lightly, but her face was grim.

Dr Farquhar produced a pocket-torch and shone a light in James's eye. 'Almost done,' he said, then switched off the torch. 'Now, do you feel sick?'

'A little,' said James.

'How's your vision?'

James paused before replying. 'Bit blurry.'

'What colour is this sheet?' He pointed at the linen on which James's hand was resting.

James frowned at it. 'It's — pale yellow?' We all eyed the white sheet. 'It shouldn't be.'

'No, it shouldn't. How's your heart feeling?'

'Like it's beating out of my chest.'

'I'm not surprised.' Dr Farquhar pulled out a little notebook and wrote rapidly. 'It's as well you stopped at one glass, young man.' He snapped the notebook shut. 'I suspect that whatever you drank was laced with digitalis. All the symptoms are tending that way.'

My eyes met Katherine's.

'You've been very lucky. Your heart rate is already — just — within the normal range. The nausea and the visual disturbances will dissipate by themselves. However, what I must prescribe is complete bed rest until your heart feels normal again.'

James's lip curled. 'How can I run a newspaper from my bed?'

'You'll find a way.' Dr Farquhar smiled at him, but the smile vanished as he caught sight of Katherine's anxious face. 'And while I'm here I'll take a look at you, Mrs King.'

'I'll be downstairs,' said Albert, rising hastily. I raised an eyebrow at Katherine, who suddenly seemed even smaller than usual, and she shook her head.

Dr Farquhar took Katherine's pulse, examined her tongue, and asked how she was sleeping. 'Are you working on a case?'

'We're always working on a case,' said Katherine.

'Then you're doing too much,' said Dr Farquhar. 'You're run down, Mrs King, and this worry won't help, especially in your current, ah, state. Don't you usually have a servant?'

'Yes, it's Susan's night off.'

'Is there another bed made up in the house?'

Katherine nodded.

'Then you will sleep there, to ensure that you get some rest and don't spend all night waiting on your husband. Mrs Lamont, may I ask you to make Mrs King a hot drink and stay until Susan returns?'

'Of course,' I said.

'In that case, I am satisfied. If anything happens to give you concern, telephone me.'

***

Somewhere outside a church clock struck one.

I had packed Albert off quite firmly. 'There's no sense in both of us staying, and Susan could be out till eleven. I'll probably sleep here, anyway.'

He seemed rather relieved as he kissed me. 'Look after yourself, Connie. And those two reprobates, of course.' He frowned. 'We haven't been sent any poisoned port, have we?'

'Not that I know of,' I replied. 'If there had been two bottles, Reg would have given us one each. He doesn't drink anything stronger than beer, and neither does Maria. She says it makes her hems crooked.'

'One less thing to worry about, then.' He kissed me again, but it was in a *goodbye* way. 'You can update me on the patients tomorrow. Sleep well.'

Susan had been horror-stricken when she arrived home at half past ten, though I delivered the news as delicately as I could. 'Oh the poor master!' she said, flinging off her coat and hat. 'And the missis, too!'

'They're both asleep, Susan,' I said.

In the spare room, half an hour before, Katherine's head had drooped over her cup of hot milk. I took it away and helped her into her nightgown. She was starting to stand and walk differently now. She caught sight of me looking, and smiled. 'It does feel so odd,' she said. 'But so right, at the same time.'

'Yes.' I pulled back the covers for her. 'Would you like me to take down your hair?'

'Are you sure?'

I picked up her brush from the dressing table. 'Of course. Come and sit down.' I took out the hairpins carefully, undid her plaits, and began brushing, easing the bristles gently through her curls.

Katherine leaned back a little, and her shoulders relaxed. 'You can come here again,' she said.

'Or you could have a maid,' I said. 'Susan does a wonderful job, but with a baby —'

'I suppose,' said Katherine, grudgingly.

'It would have been much easier tonight.'

Her shoulders tensed. 'I didn't ask you to come.'

'Don't be silly. I don't mind at all. But one maid, for a house this size, and you still haven't found a cook. You can't keep helping with the housework...' I got to one hundred, and divided Katherine's hair into three thick strands.

She was watching me in the mirror. I kept my eyes on her growing plait.

'Maybe you could discuss it with James when he's feeling a bit better.' Holding the end of the plait tightly, I leaned over Katherine to get a ribbon from the table.

'Maybe.' She closed her eyes. 'I hope he doesn't have to stay in bed long. He'll be fidgety, and unbearable —'

'You can worry about that in the morning.' I tied her plait and waved the end in front of her face. 'Will that do, madam?'

'Very nice,' said Katherine. 'You're hired.'

I helped her into bed and gave her the mug of milk to finish. 'So much to think about,' she murmured, as I took the mug and adjusted her pillows.

'Not now,' I whispered. 'In the morning.'

James blinked at the light from the landing when I went in to him. 'Sorry, did I wake you?' I murmured.

He shook his head. 'Heart's still pounding.'

'And you're worrying about it.'

'Well, yes.' I could hear it in his voice.

'Shall I read to you?'

'It's worth a try.' James resettled himself in the bed with a great deal of humphing and bashing of pillows. *Poor*

Katherine, I thought. 'Something really dull.'

I spied the *Times* lying on a nearby chair. *Hmm.* I picked it up and riffled through it until I came to the financial section. 'Stock prices,' I read.

'I can't wait to find out how it ends,' said James.

I droned through the lists of items; cotton per bale, and jute, and silk in all varieties; gold, silver, tin, copper —

Cautious on copper flashed into my head, for no reason —

Corn, wheat, maize, per ton…

'Who needs a ton of maize?' murmured James, and yawned.

'These are the current share prices according to the London Stock Exchange…' I kept an eye on James as I read. He seemed to sink into the bed, and his breathing grew more regular. *There.* I rose, and left quietly.

And now here I was, dressed in a pair of James's pyjamas (the only nightwear in the house which would fit me), wrapped in a blanket on the parlour sofa and too full of thoughts to sleep. Susan had offered her bed, but I had a feeling she would need a good night's rest more than I, for she would have James, Katherine, and a house to look after the next day.

Who had sent the port?

'From a satisfied customer,' the label had said. Dr Farquhar had taken the bottle away for analysis — had he taken the label, too? I sighed, extricated myself from the blanket, and snapped on the light switch. No, there it was on the sideboard. It was handwritten in squarish capitals using blue ink and, from the look of it, a dip pen.

Not the same writing. Not the same person.

But their scheme had misfired. The port, clearly, had been meant for Katherine and I. We were supposed to open it, toast each other, and collapse in the office.

I almost laughed. As if Katherine and I would have a glass of port in the office!

James, on the other hand, had made a beeline for it. So it must have been good port — in fact, nicer than whatever he usually drank. And the remaining bottle certainly looked eminently respectable.

So whoever had sent the port had access to an excellent bottle, but did not understand that Katherine and I were unlikely to drink it, and definitely not then and there.

I found paper and pen and scribbled a note to myself: *Find out what kind of port — vintage? Would James remember? Otherwise ask Dr F.*

Someone who didn't go to formal dinners? Or who didn't know the usual customs for drinking alcohol? I scribbled my thoughts, then left the note with the label and sat on the sofa, the blanket over my cold feet.

Two different people trying to harm us. A note for Evangeline, and poison for Katherine and me.

I sighed, and swung my legs up. Perhaps Margaret's Mr Taplow would end up analysing the port. I must remember to ask her about it in the morning... I yawned. And see what Reg had found out about the elusive Mr Latimer, whose shop, again, had been closed when I had visited that afternoon. *I wonder he can sell a thing*, I thought. *How does he manage for money? I wonder if...* But my thoughts wouldn't untangle themselves.

A tap on the door woke me. 'Come in!' I called, struggling into a sitting position.

Susan poked her head round the door. 'Would you like tea, ma'am?' she asked. She appeared bright and well-rested, while I was fairly confident that I did not.

'Please,' I said.

'That'll make you feel *much* better,' said Susan. 'Once you've had a bit of breakfast you can go home and have a proper rest.'

'I should go and check on —'

'No need,' said Susan. 'I've peeped in on them both, and they're still fast asleep. Master looks well.' She sounded almost accusing, as if we might have exaggerated the whole thing. 'Anyway, I'll leave you to get dressed, and bring tea in ten minutes.'

'Thank you.' I groaned as I got up. My bones ached, and some of them seemed to have changed places in the night. I got into my clothes somehow, and repaired to the bathroom to tidy myself. I looked as if I hadn't slept a wink. Albert would probably tell me off, and — I groaned again as I thought of the discussion I still hadn't had.

My plait had come loose in the night. Without a brush I couldn't do much; but I re-plaited the lower half and secured it more tightly with the ribbon. *Loose ends*, I thought, frowning at my washed-out reflection. *Loose ends everywhere.*

Chapter 17
Katherine

The clink of china woke me. A sense of panic descended and for a second I couldn't remember why.

'I must...'

'No you mustn't, Mrs Kitty. You stay put,' ordered Ada's voice. I heard the swish of her skirts as she strode across the room to open the curtains. Fog sneaked round the edges of the sash and sucked the glass.

'But James...'

'He's doing very well and you needn't worry. Miss Margaret is practising on him.'

'Oh dear.' I tried to push back the covers, but Ada sat on the edge of the bed, trapping me. I considered trying to escape on the other side but suspected she'd be quicker.

Ada's eyes twinkled and she patted my hand before putting a wrap round me. 'Don't worry, an actual doctor is here.'

'You mean a man.'

She scowled at me. 'For shame, Mrs Kitty. I mean trained. In fact, there are two. Mrs Lamont's Dr Farquhar and your Dr Nicholls. Miss Margaret asked her to come in case "old-fashioned medicine" made too much fuss of both of you. And here's me, with no training whatsoever, saying don't get up till you've had a cup of tea and a biscuit, or else. One of *my* biscuits, not one of Susan's efforts.'

'Where's Connie?'

'Mrs Lamont has gone home, bless her.' A soft smile crossed her face. 'Wouldn't wait for breakfast once she knew I was here to manage things. She's missing those children something rotten, I'll wager. As for you, eat a biscuit. I'm going to teach Susan how to make a proper breakfast and I'm staying in this house till you've got a proper cook. You shouldn't be going out every night eating foreign stuff in your condition. Good bit of boiled beef is what you need.'

I wasn't allowed to visit James until I had been seen by both doctors, who argued politely about expectant mothers but agreed light exercise was best, provided I stayed inside out of the fog. Finally, dressed for a day at home, I was able to see how he was.

'Why am I on bed rest?' he said. 'You're up and gallivanting even though you're starting to look like you've swallowed a cushion.'

'Such flattery,' I gave his hand a mock slap. 'At least I don't look half-dead. You shouldn't swig strong spirits in preference to cocoa.'

'It was a good bottle.' A reminiscent grin was replaced by a slight frown. He rubbed his chin. 'But there's something about it...' He stopped and looked at me. Somehow I could guess what was coming.

'Are you getting tired?' He shook his head. 'What is it?'

Margaret wandered into the room and sat on the end of the bed.

'Doctors aren't supposed to do that,' I pointed out.

'Like I told you,' she said, 'I'm going into research — poisons. It's very considerate of James to be helping.'

'What was it, James?' I said. 'What were you going to say about the bottle?'

'It was a particular vintage. There was one just like it in Lion House. I took it back to Hazelgrove, remember? Miss Q had more than one type of port in that pantry and originally many more than two bottles of everything. Judging from the inventory, the wine-cellar is, like the silverware collection, rather depleted. But I'm sure it's the same type.'

'That's ridiculous,' said Margaret. 'The only client connected with Lion House is —'

'Evangeline,' said James. 'That's what I told Connie. She wondered if the anonymous letter was accusing Evangeline of murder for gain. But even if she could, she wouldn't,' said James. 'My sister has no need of money and she was fond of the old bird. I mean, she wouldn't even step on a beetle, and then Connie said something about . . . someone knowing about Evangeline's prospects who couldn't . . . something.' James ran his hand through his hair. 'She looked totally exhausted. I couldn't grasp what she meant but she seemed agitated, as if she had a hundred things on her mind at once and didn't know what to think.'

'*And* she's got to go to lunch at Uncle Maurice's.' Margaret pulled a face. 'She'd completely forgotten. I barely had time to speak to her before she rushed off — you know how particular he is about punctuality. Three of the cousins will be there and Uncle Maurice does so criticise them. She looked as if she'd rather jump in the Thames than go.'

'Which ones, apart from Albert?' I said.

'Moss and Douglas,' said Margaret. 'The "disappointments". At least Albert managed to get married *and* produce an heir.'

James was blinking more and more, as if he were about to fall asleep, and I kissed him before beckoning Margaret away to the sitting room.

'What's for lunch?' she asked as we entered.

'Baked ham,' I said. 'It may be a while, Ada is trying to teach Susan and didn't start till late. Are you especially hungry?'

'Not at all. But I wish I could have told Connie about last night.'

'Why Connie and not me?' I was hurt.

'Because she'd be listening rather than worrying whether my honour had been compromised.'

'She'd worry just as much.'

'No-one worries as much as you and pretends they don't. Still, you'll have to do.' She stood and peered out of the window. It was unlike her not to rush straight into what she was thinking. She looked as unsettled as I felt.

'Would you come with me to the office?' I asked.

Margaret turned from the window to frown at me. 'What for?'

'Ada's here to mind James and I can tell you everything on the way.'

'You're supposed to be resting. And the weather's filthy.'

'Come on, Margaret. I can put a scarf over my face or hold my breath when we're outside. It won't take long, and we can bring the anonymous letter back. Will you hail a cab for us?'

A conspiratorial grin flashed across her face.

'I thought you probably wouldn't say no,' I said, but I felt guilty the whole way to the office. The fog made everything look as if it were being viewed through yellow glass. The rattling wheels, shouts, and swearing as the traffic tangled up were muffled and distant.

'I didn't mean it about being glad James had been poisoned,' Margaret said. 'Dr F says that he thinks the amount in the port was tiny. If James had drunk the whole bottle it might have been different.'

'It may be that the person who sent it doesn't realise most people don't drink port that way. Not to mention that it's generally a gentleman's drink.'

'That rules out Evangeline,' said Margaret. 'She'd know.'

'Unless it was done to warn rather than to kill.'

Margaret's eyes flashed. 'You can't think Evangeline would hurt anyone.'

'Of course I don't. She's not the only person to know about port. Just because it was a bottle like the one in Lion House doesn't mean it came from there. Other people will have bought them for their houses, restaurants, hotels and so on. We shall enquire of the wine merchants as soon as Dr Farquhar returns the bottle.'

'It's a shame I can't give it to Frank,' said Margaret. 'He could show me how to do the analysis.'

'Talking of Frank —'

'Oh yes.' Margaret took a deep breath. Despite the slow-moving traffic, we were nearly at the office. 'Dinner was nice. French. Consommé, daube of beef and Charlotte Russe. Rather dreary wallpaper.'

'Never mind dinner.'

'I'm just setting the scene.'

'Never mind the scene, what about the conversation?'

'I'm beautiful and wonderful and should be treated like a princess.'

'*Everyone* knows that,' I said. 'You've been telling us ever since you could talk. What else?'

'His sister doesn't approve of his connection to me, which is quite satisfying. I've never been considered disreputable before. To be truthful —' She bit her lip. 'I think it's more that she wants to distance herself from the village and has a low opinion of Evangeline. Frank asked how I felt about her and I confess I made a vague response with my eyes on my plate, which he took to mean I was too polite to say I didn't like her either. Then he said maybe I'd be acceptable after all. The utter *cheek*. It was all I could do to flutter my eyelashes at him rather than punch him, and say I admired resourceful women like his sister although it was a shame she and I had to work for a living. Which is *tosh*, but needs must.'

I grinned, imagining Margaret's gritted teeth.

'He's ashamed that either of them have to work but their poor father lost *all* the family money to *utter blackguards* — his words — leaving only a house which they had to sell in order to buy a flat and release some cash. It must have been a total ruin. His salary just pays the bills but he's proud Mary didn't have to *stoop* to being a governess.' Margaret rolled her eyes. 'He says that in the periodicals she reads a companion is considered far superior. And it's simply *shocking* that after the loyalty Mary had given three old ladies, the two who died left her nothing of note, and the one in the middle who didn't die gave her an old marquetry box as a parting gift. Mary is convinced that Evangeline manipulated Miss Quinton into changing the will.'

'Did you ask about last Christmas?'

'There were men or a man — Mr Latimer certainly — who spent time shut up with Miss Quinton, and Evangeline made more visits than usual. Or that's what Mary thinks. Miss Quinton cooled towards Mary Taplow after that and she thought there must be a connection. The servants of course were *always* disrespectful and Mary had to make them know their place. That's it. Anyway, here we are.' Margaret asked the cabbie to wait and helped me out onto the pavement. Pedestrians blinded by mufflers and fog bumped into us, and a tall man stood on my foot, his damp overcoat pressing for a second against my face as he passed. Margaret stabbed outwards with her umbrella and made us a path to the door.

In the office, Reg looked up in surprise. He was sitting

with his feet on the desk, reading a letter.

'Wondered where you'd got to,' he said. 'Thought maybe you'd downed the whole bottle and had a bit of a head.'

'I'm sorry, Reg,' I said. 'I should have let you know.' I gave a brief explanation and asked him what he was reading.

Reg was so upset that he flung his arms round me before he remembered propriety.

'Mr King will be fine,' I said. 'It's not your fault. Now what's the letter?'

'It's from the Monsarrat Agency,' said Reg. 'I've been enquiring about kitchen staff. It's taken three goes, cos I had to be very specific before they sent information about Mrs Booth. All I want now is someone who needs a good cook.'

Margaret caught my eye. 'Katherine does,' she said.

CHAPTER 18
Connie

'Connie, stop fussing. You look lovely.'

'I look exhausted.' I screwed my earring in a little more tightly. Violet had done her best; but despite a long hot bath and my new day dress I was still tired and glum. For the first time I thought longingly of the boxes of powder and rouge at the music hall. I certainly needed something to brighten me up.

'It's only a family lunch. None of them will even notice.'

'I'll know, though.'

Albert detached himself from the doorway and offered me a hand. 'You need a break from all this, Connie.'

I sighed. 'Perhaps I do.' I scrutinised him as I got to my feet. There was a little crease between his eyebrows which wasn't usually there. 'So do you, I think.'

A sharp glance at me, then away again. 'We'll be late if you don't hurry.'

Albert looked out of the carriage window most of the

way to the family home in Belgravia. *If this is a break from detective work*, I thought, *I'd rather be in the office.*

Or in the nursery. Bee had greeted me with extravagant hugs, crying 'Mama! We thought you was lost!'

'Were lost,' I corrected automatically, before laughing and scooping her up. 'No, Auntie Katherine was unwell, and I stayed to look after her.'

Bee pouted. 'I couldn't sleep,' she said. 'Wanted Mama to say goodnight.'

'Oh, Bee...' I put her down and stroked her hair. 'I'll come and say goodnight and tuck you in tonight, I promise. Well, unless —'

Bee's plump little hands clenched.

'I'll try my very best,' I said, but she had already picked up a doll, hugging it tightly to her.

'Has Nanny written again yet?' I asked Lily, who looked much as I felt.

'She says her sister is much better, and she should be able to return soon,' said Lily, faintly. I made up my mind to give her a holiday once the nursery had returned to some sort of order.

We were in the quiet leafy squares of Belgravia now, and Tredwell slowed the horses almost to walking pace as we approached the Lamont residence. That was how I always thought of Albert's family home, though I supposed our house could be described the same way.

Buck yourself up, Connie, I told myself.

But truthfully the Lamont residence was the last place I wished to be. For I knew that, as well as Albert's father, Moss would be there.

Moss, who had a plausible reason for sending the anonymous letter to Evangeline.

Moss, who was trying to get fast money out of my husband.

Moss, who —

I shook my head until my earrings jangled. I couldn't believe that of him.

But Moss knows his port, a little voice insisted.

***

'Come in, come in!' Albert's father was standing in the hall as the door opened to us, and I suspected he had been waiting for our arrival. 'I don't know what time you call this, B — Albert. You've barely got time for a sherry.'

'Sorry, Father,' said Albert. 'Connie was held up in the nursery seeing to George.'

'Ah, George!' Mr Lamont beamed. 'How is the son and heir? Thriving, I trust.'

'Growing every day,' said Albert.

'I'm not surprised,' said Mr Lamont, chuckling. 'You were a long thin child, and Connie is a fine tall woman.' He glanced at me appraisingly, and I tried not to feel like a horse being assessed at the county fair.

'Bee is shooting up too,' I remarked, as Dinsdale hurried over with a tray of drinks. 'No thank you, I'll wait until dinner.' Albert took a glass, and I watched him narrowly as he sipped. 'Are the others here?'

'Oh yes, Moss and Dougie have been sat down half an hour. Taking advantage of the old man's cellar, what.' Mr Lamont led the way into the dining room, and I took the opportunity to grimace while he couldn't see me.

I straightened my face hastily as the men rose. Douglas was built on the general Lamont pattern, being tall, broad and red of face. Moss looked like a sapling next to a stout oak. 'Connie,' he said, and nodded to me.

'Hullo again, Moss,' I said. 'We almost met the other day, remember?'

Moss frowned. 'Ha, very good,' he said, eventually. 'I was somewhat preoccupied.'

'Preoccupation shouldn't get in the way of politeness, Moss,' chided Mr Lamont, subsiding into his carver chair at the head of the table.

'That it shouldn't, Father.' Moss took his seat on Mr Lamont's right.

Mr Lamont regarded him. 'What have you got to be preoccupied about? The last I heard, Albert was managing your affairs. You're like a lily of the field, Moss. You toil not.' He laughed so hard that he began to cough. 'Take your seats, everyone,' he choked out, tossing back the rest of his sherry.

At least, as such a small party, we were not observing formal dining rules. I would not have had two words to say to Douglas, who sat stolidly demolishing his fillet of sole, then fidgeting while the rest of us finished. 'He's waiting for the beef, aren't you, lad!' chortled Mr Lamont. Douglas, as far as I knew, still lived at home, and I wondered how many times he had heard this remark.

A joint duly arrived and Mr Lamont did the honours, carving off thick slices while the parlourmaids helped us to vegetables. I thought of Mrs Jones and Nancy and Johnson at home, and thanked Providence that Albert required no such elaborate arrangement. A decanter of red wine was brought, and glasses filled. All the Lamonts had excellent appetites, and scarcely drew breath until plates were clean. Jugged hare followed, of which I accepted a small portion. 'You need to keep your strength up, Connie,' observed Mr Lamont, tucking in. 'You've got an army to raise.' He glanced at Albert inquiringly.

'How are things with you, Moss?' I asked, in an attempt to turn the conversation.

'Oh, so-so,' said Moss, smiling briefly and unconvincingly before addressing himself to his plate again.

'I believe young Moss here has thoughts of matrimony,' said Mr Lamont, winking at me. 'About time too, hey?'

'To everything there is a season,' said Moss stiffly. 'Let me help you to more wine, Father.' He reached for the decanter, which had been left on the table for ease, and filled Mr Lamont's glass.

'There may be,' said Mr Lamont, taking up the glass, 'but he's as close as an oyster about it.'

'I don't believe in being hasty,' said Moss. I raised my eyebrows, remembering the conversation I had overheard in the study, and noted that Moss was very deliberately not looking in my direction. Or Albert's.

'That was a splendid meal,' said Albert, putting his knife and fork together.

'We're not done yet.' Mr Lamont turned to the footman standing behind him. 'Bring in the pudding!'

My heart sank. A steaming pudding came in, flaming with brandy, and a parlourmaid bore a jug of custard. But there was also a plate of delicate fruit tartlets, and I selected one of those and a spoonful of cream, feeling that honour had been satisfied. Even so, it took me a few minutes to finish it, so full was I.

'You two should hurry up and get married,' said Mr Lamont, frowning at Moss and Douglas. 'With Connie the only woman, we can hardly banish her to the drawing room and send the port round, can we?'

'I really don't mind,' I said, putting my napkin on the table.

Mr Lamont motioned me back into my seat. 'Brandy for me,' he said, and two decanters were soon in motion round the table. 'We won't smoke,' he said resignedly. 'D'ye want coffee?' I assented, in the hope that it would keep me awake at least until we could go home.

Conversation languished, and soon each Lamont was looking thoughtfully at their half-finished drink, while Mr Lamont's head sunk lower and lower till he straightened up with a jerk. 'That was a lunch, wasn't it?' He grinned round the table. 'You're all half asleep!'

'I think we are.' Albert got up and patted his father on the shoulder. 'It's been very nice, Father.'

'Good, good,' said Mr Lamont, slipping a little in his chair. 'Good to see you, Bertie. Keep up the good work, eh?'

'I should head off, too,' said Moss, rising.

'Business to take care of, eh?' Mr Lamont wheezed with laughter. 'Be off with you, boy.'

***

Albert and I groaned as the carriage jerked over a loose

cobble, then laughed at each other's dismayed faces.

'I don't think I've ever eaten so much,' I said.

Albert stroked his waistcoat. 'I'm out of practice. Four courses at lunch is a tall order. Father will probably sleep all afternoon.' Suddenly he slid along the seat and put an arm round me. 'I'm sorry I've been a bit — absent lately.'

'Is that the brandy talking?' I asked, snuggling up.

He grinned down at me. 'Maybe a bit...' His face grew serious. 'Connie, your father has asked me to, um, take a bit more of a hand in the family business.'

'Oh.' I drew back a little to look at him. 'Is there a reason?'

He kissed my forehead. 'Don't be so suspicious, Connie,' he murmured. 'Nothing particular. He just says he's getting a bit long in the tooth.'

I considered this. 'Well, he's fifty-eight next birthday, and ever since I can remember he's been closeted either in his study or the office in the City.' I looked up at Albert again. 'Will that be you?'

'I hope not.' Albert smoothed a lock of hair off my forehead. 'I'm examining all the angles to make sure that it isn't.'

'So that's why you've been shut up in the study, and going to all those meetings.' A weight lifted from me.

'Mm-hm.' He lifted my chin to kiss me properly. 'I wasn't sure how to tell you. I thought it might worry you.'

I kissed him back. 'I trust you.'

At home we let Nancy know that, having lunched too well, we would rather not be disturbed for a couple of hours. 'I see, sir, ma'am,' she said, grinning. 'Shall I call you at six?'

'Yes please,' I said. 'Tell Mrs Jones not to worry about dinner for us. I'm not even sure about supper, at present.'

Our orders given, we settled down for a well-earned rest.

Tap-tap-tap-tap-tap. I blinked, but the insistent knocking continued. 'What is it? Who's there?'

'I'm so sorry, ma'am, may I come in?' Johnson's voice, apologetic.

I nudged Albert. 'Yes, come in.'

Johnson sidled round the door. 'I know you said not to be disturbed —'

'We're awake now,' I said, 'what's the matter?'

'A telegram has come, and the boy's waiting —'

He was looking at Albert. Albert sat up, took it from his hand, and ripped it open. I peered over his shoulder.

Father unwell STOP Unresponsive STOP Doctor on way STOP Please come STOP Douglas

CHAPTER 19
Katherine

'But she'd recognise me,' I said.

'Does that matter?' argued Margaret.

I pondered. Mrs Booth might not be so open to Evangeline's sister-in-law, assuming that she had paid any attention to me. And if she was straining at the bit in a country house in Berkshire, why would she be interested in a smaller establishment in Bayswater? To date, our dinner parties had been informal. More often than not our guests included music-hall performers or characters collected by James. If necessary we would bring in a hired cook, and on other occasions everyone endured what Susan and I could cobble together, or picnicked on delights from Fortnum's or curious food shops in Soho. Connie would be a better choice; but quite apart from what would happen if Mrs Jones got wind of the matter and misunderstood, Connie didn't need another domestic thing to worry about.

'You're getting married,' I told Margaret.

'I'm certainly not.'

'You are for the purpose of interviewing Mrs Booth. Someone can pretend to be your mother. We need a grand enough house — oh! I know exactly where.'

'Who am I supposed to be marrying?'

'Whomever you please.'

'I'm still free, Miss,' said Reg. 'Better snap me up quick.'

'Are you? I thought you were too busy contemplating the lilies of the field.' I raised my eyebrows at him and he blushed. 'In the meantime, can you write to the agency and ask if Mrs Booth can attend for interview with Miss Demeray on Friday at this address?' I scribbled it down.

'Oh!' he said. 'Fancy.' Then he chuckled. 'She'll be up for it.'

'Come *on*, Katherine,' said my sister. 'That cab bill will be shocking. Let's go back before James drags himself out of his sick bed to look for you.'

The fog if anything was thicker than before, the cab just about discernible at the kerb. As I pulled my muffler over my mouth and nose, I was jostled. This time more forcibly, as if with intent. The man was tall and broad, his face obscured as mine was. He spoke but I couldn't make out his words. Margaret pushed him and, finding her arm grabbed at, struck him not only with the umbrella but her bag, while tripping him with her foot. As he fell Margaret steered me towards the cab.

'Where's the driver?' Her voice was panicked. The man on the pavement had become tangled with passers-by, all of whom were more intent on cursing him rather than helping him, but the cabbie was nowhere to be seen.

'Quick!' Margaret urged. 'You can drive a trap, it can't be that different. Let's go before he comes after us.' She pushed me towards the driver's seat and climbed up behind me. With a backward glance at our assailant, I clicked at the horse and pulled into the stream of traffic. This was nothing like a Berkshire lane. Other vehicles came from every direction, cutting across, coming head-on. Bicycles whizzed in and out, and pedestrians flung themselves off the pavement, which was all the more unnerving because they were invisible until the last moment.

'Hey! Come back!' a male voice shouted after us.

'Is that the cabbie?' I said, my hands shaking on the reins.

'No,' said Margaret. 'It's the man outside the office. Come on, hurry up.'

'How?'

'Wot the — blazes do you think you're doing?' Another voice, closer at hand, bellowed at us. Margaret twisted.

'Oh dear,' she said. 'I've found the cabbie. He was inside. I'm sorry, it's us. We just wanted to get home and we thought you'd gone. We'll pay the whole fare.'

'Stop this flaming cab right now. Don't make me have to climb out.'

'I'm not sure I can,' I whispered.

'I think he's climbing out,' Margaret whispered back. She turned and called, 'I'm sorry, there was a man —'

'Do you know where you're even blooming going? Cos if you're trying to get back where you come from you're going the wrong way. Pull over, else it'll take hours to get right. So help me, women! Five minutes out of the fog and I get kidnapped in my own cab! Here Hannibal! Whoa there! Whoa!'

At the sound of someone who knew what he was doing the horse came to an abrupt stop. There was a bang and a curse as a bicycle crashed into the back. The cabbie, after swearing at it, turned to us, counted to ten and helped us down.

'There was this man...' stated Margaret.

The cabbie helped me alight with more gentleness. 'And you in your condition,' he said. 'Wot you thinking of?'

'There *was*...' Margaret persisted.

A cyclist came up, wheeling a damaged bicycle. He pulled down his muffler and doffed his cap. It was Inspector Havelock. 'All I wanted to do was speak to you. You were coming out of your office as I arrived, and rushed off. And now I'm black and blue and my wheel is bent.'

***

James, who had won a battle with Ada for once and was sitting in his armchair wrapped in blankets, was less than impressed even by the edited version of events. I hadn't told him about the cabbie's bill which included trespass, kidnap, damage by bicycle, and carriage of said bicycle along with Inspector Havelock. Susan patched up the latter's grazes. Her face red, she asked if he'd like her to mend the tear in his trousers. With a smile, he declined; but he accepted an invitation to lunch.

I perhaps shouldn't have been surprised when James

told him about the port and his suspicions. 'The bottle is with Dr Farquhar,' he said. 'I know he was about to report the matter himself. The police may have more resources to trace its origins and where it might have been sold. Lion House is just one possibility, but we can't discount it.'

'Thank you Mr King, I appreciate your openness.' He turned to me. 'And you, Mrs King? Have Misses Caster and Fleet managed to find anything pertinent?'

Evangeline's accusing anonymous letter and the ones in foreign script still lurked in the file in Margaret's bag, along with notes about Mr Latimer. None of it amounted to anything. Inspector Havelock was not a complete fool . . . but if I were to give him our vague suspicions, he would think *I* was.

'There may be a link to classical art,' I said. 'It's all we have so far. James, was everything of that nature in the inventory accounted for?'

James snorted. 'Ah, the inventory. Or as I like to call it, the list of the missing.'

***

By tea-time, when the inspector had long gone, everyone including the baby, who had seemed to enjoy the morning's exertions, had settled into a doze. When the telephone rang and I heard Connie's tearful voice, I assumed she was calling to say she was too tired to visit, and I was ready to tell her not to worry when her words started to sink in. I couldn't answer. I heard her calling 'Katherine! Katherine!' but a million thoughts churned through my mind before I could speak. Uncle Maurice was dead. I loved that irascible, stubborn but underneath it all family man. I remembered Mother telling me that he had never been the same after my aunt died, happy for Mother to take Albert under her wing, willing to keep Margaret in school when I'd feared she'd lose the opportunities she deserved. I remembered him walking me down the aisle, stooping to whisper 'I know it's not me you want, but I'm proud to stand in his place.' The tears ran down my cheeks and I still couldn't speak.

***

It was three days before Connie and I could find the time or ability to talk about the case. The office felt like a refuge from the tears and rearrangements but not from the grief. The funeral had been held, the will read. Margaret and I had been remembered with small bequests.

'I hate black,' said Connie. 'And I'll be stuck in it for ages. It's not as if it'll bring him back or make Albert smile.'

'How are the Lamonts faring?'

'Well…' Connie paused. 'I sense there's some resentment towards Moss for getting the house and much of the capital, but at least he was the eldest. There's more towards Albert for getting a higher proportion of the remainder than his siblings. But Moss is distraught.'

'That might explain why he hasn't written to Evangeline. She asked me to see if he was all right. I've explained about Uncle Maurice.'

'I can't bear to talk about him any more.' Connie sighed and opened up the folder I'd brought back from my house. I wasn't sure if she meant Moss or Uncle Maurice. 'Have the police said any more about the port?'

'Not so far. I'm hoping they've found the vintner and are going through the records to identify the destination of that particular batch. I was resentful James didn't leave that with us at first, but I'm glad now.'

'At least he is getting better,' she said. 'How are you?'

'I'm fine and so is the baby,' I said. 'And I don't believe for one moment it will turn out miserable because of this. I do run out of breath when I rush though.'

'Don't rush then.' Connie picked up the notes on Mr Latimer, and sighed. 'This has been one of the worst weeks of my life and now I'm afraid — I mean, I believe we should go to Brompton. I fancy some fine art.'

Connie didn't look like she fancied anything, but relieved to be distracted from thinking about Uncle Maurice, I gathered my things and followed. I was paying too little attention to notice that she had changed the subject again.

CHAPTER 20
Connie

Once the carriage set off I managed to keep up a stream of bright chatter for approximately five minutes before Katherine interrupted me. 'Connie, what's wrong?'

'Wrong? Nothing's wrong. It's a lovely late-autumn day and we're on the trail of stolen antiques.'

Katherine sighed. 'And you're determined not to let me get a word in edgeways. Connie, I can tell when you're trying not to think about something, and from the way you're gabbling, you don't want to tell me about it either.'

She looked at me very steadily. I was glad I hadn't had Katherine as a sister, growing up, because she would have been able to read my thoughts far too easily. I gazed out of the window to escape, but I could *feel* her looking.

'It's Moss,' I said, to a passing lamp-post.

Katherine moved closer and touched my arm. 'What do you mean?'

'I'm worried about Moss.'

'Moss will be fine. He's upset, of course he is, but he'll get used to being master of the house, and the family will get used to it too. Perhaps in a few months he'll propose to Evangeline, and then they'll both be happy.'

I couldn't do it. I couldn't say what was in my mind. 'Yes.' That was all I could manage without lying to my dearest friend. Instead I fished the Lion House inventory out of my bag and studied it for the remainder of the journey.

***

Mr Latimer's shop, which I had visited several times in vain, had seen better days. The paint on the frame of the large plate-glass window was flaking, and the sign was faded. However the shop was, at last, open, and the lights in the windows illuminated an impressive array of statuary.

Katherine narrowed her eyes at it. 'Some of that is very Lion House-ish.'

'It is, rather.' I nudged her. 'How shall we play it?'

'Interested buyers, I think,' said Katherine. 'We can always turn official later.'

A bell jangled as I pushed the door open, which surprised me. It made the shop seem no different from a grocer's or a butcher's, whose bells I had often heard ring. A slim, dark man of indeterminate age, dressed in a good suit, came to meet us. 'Good afternoon, ladies,' he said, bowing over my hand. 'Are you looking for anything in particular today?'

'I'm not quite sure what I want,' I said. 'I'm interested in sculpture, but my husband wishes to make sure it's a good investment.'

'Ahh.' He smiled at me in a slightly conspiratorial way. 'So we need to find something which will please you and satisfy him.'

I beamed. 'That's exactly it,' I said. 'Is this your shop?'

He bowed slightly. 'It is, madam.'

'Then you must be an extremely good judge of art and antiques.' I moved a little closer. *Nice to meet you at last, Mr Latimer.*

'What about this one?' asked Katherine, indicating a statue of a nymph placed in the centre of the window. Her right arm had broken off at the wrist, but the carving was exquisite.

'Madam has an eye,' said Mr Latimer. 'She is a very nice piece indeed, and dates from the second century AD. She is Roman.'

'Good heavens,' I said. 'Are you sure?'

'Oh yes.' He smirked. 'I have a statement of provenance.'

'How wonderful,' I breathed. 'Where did you find her?'

Mr Latimer brushed a speck from his sleeve. 'I have a network of suppliers,' he said, oh so casually. 'This piece came from a great house in Berkshire.'

It was on the tip of my tongue to ask which, but I was conscious of Katherine's warning look. I contented myself with admiring the nymph, who appeared rather chilly in her scant draperies, truth be told. 'She is beautiful,' I murmured. 'My husband would love her. He reads Virgil in the original, and everything.'

'If that style is agreeable to you,' purred Mr Latimer, 'I could show you other items from the same house.'

I glanced at Katherine. 'That would be delightful.'

***

We left the shop without any purchases, but with a scribbled list of items for me to show my investment-minded Latin-reading husband, complete with dates and original locations, and Mr Latimer's card. 'I'm often out of the shop,' he said, as he put the card into my hand and gently closed my gloved fingers over it. 'However, you can always reach me by letter or wire here.' The card read *Augustus Latimer, Esq*, and the address was Wright Terrace.

'We'll have to go through the list properly in the office,' said Katherine, eyeing the darkening sky as we got back into the carriage.

'Successful trip?' asked Tredwell.

'Very much so,' Katherine replied.

'Where next? Marylebone? Bayswater?'

'The office, please.'

Tredwell said nothing, and clicked to the horses.

'I don't think he approves,' said Katherine, settling against the cushions.

'It isn't up to him.'

Katherine was giving me the steady look again. 'What did you think of Mr L?'

I considered. 'Younger than I imagined. More charming than I imagined. If you like that sort of thing.'

'You certainly appeared to,' said Katherine, grinning.

'That was an act,' I said, frostily. 'Slim, dark, graceful. He sounded English, but I don't think he is, entirely.'

'No,' said Katherine. 'I wonder —'

I raised my eyebrows, but she shook her head. 'I need to consult something first, before I make any assumptions.' She looked as if she saw for miles. Then her gaze focused on me, and she frowned. 'I wish you'd tell me what's wrong, Connie. You were very good in the shop just now, but I *know* there's something you aren't telling me.'

I stared at her in dismay. Pregnancy had not dulled Katherine's perceptions at all; she was still as sharp as a terrier. And as tenacious.

'I'm not sure I'm right —'

'*Tell* me.' Katherine put her hand on mine. 'You look as if the world were about to fall on your head.'

'That's exactly how I feel,' I choked out. 'Ask Tredwell to stop somewhere — somewhere we won't be overheard.'

'But we're going to the office,' said Katherine.

'Reg might be there,' I murmured. 'And I'm not sure I can hold out that long.'

Katherine drew up the shade and peered outside. When she spoke her voice seemed to come through a fog. 'Is that Hyde Park, Tredwell?'

'It is, ma'am,' he called back.

'Can you pull up? We'd like a little walk.'

Katherine put her arm through mine and we strolled towards the bandstand. The park was quiet, with only a few dog-walkers braving the crisp clear air. We gained the empty bandstand, and sat down.

'You're worried about Moss,' said Katherine, simply. 'But not in the way I thought you meant.'

'No —' And it all poured out in hasty, half-gasped whispers. Moss's motive to send the anonymous letter to

Evangeline, and push her into marrying him. Moss's hasty trip to our house, to try and push Albert into boosting his funds. Moss refilling his father's glass at the lunch table —

'You don't mean —' Katherine's face showed utter horror.

'You weren't there. Mr Lamont was so down on Moss and Douglas, and so nice to Albert, and so interested in George. "The son and heir", he called him. Moss might have done it because he was worried his father might change the will in George's favour. I don't know how, but —' It dawned on me. 'He and Douglas were alone in the dining room when we came.'

Katherine's face became very serious.

'The port,' I whispered. 'The port sent to us. He would know that we wouldn't open it, and whoever did would only have a little. It was a warning to give up the case.'

'Nooooooo...' Katherine put her hands over her face. I dreaded to think what expression lay beneath, as I filled her ears with poison.

'I hate it too. I don't want to believe it. But —' There was one thing left, one final, horrible thing. 'He was at Hazelgrove the day Miss Quinton died. And he went for a walk into the village, do you remember? To buy tobacco. James and Albert both offered him some of theirs, but he said he wanted fresh air after the train.'

Katherine's shoulders shook. 'Oh, Connie... I can't believe it.'

'We have no proof,' I said.

'No, but —'

'I'm sorry.' I released her gently. 'I should have kept it

to myself.'

'You'd have exploded.'

'Perhaps.' I gave her another, gentle squeeze. 'Thank you for listening. But I'm still sorry.'

Katherine sighed. 'If Reg is still in the office let's send him home for the day,' she said. 'We need to talk it through, with strong tea.'

'I think you're right.' We walked back to the carriage as if Tredwell were our executioner.

***

'How odd,' said Katherine, as Tredwell pulled up outside our building. A policeman was there talking to several people, who were shaking their heads.

'Let me go and see.' I got out, and the policeman, whom I recognised, waved to me. 'What is it?' I asked.

'I'm so sorry, Miss Fleet, but there's been a break-in.'

Suddenly it was hard to breathe. 'Our office?' I muttered.

'I'm afraid so,' he said. 'Another officer's upstairs, taking a statement from your Reg.'

I ran to the carriage. 'We've been burgled,' I cried.

A look of fury came over Katherine's face, and she wrenched at the door handle.

***

We found the office turned upside down, and Reg wearing a shamefaced expression. 'I got a telegram from Miss Fleet,' he said. 'To check Miss Taplow's date of birth at Somerset House, urgent. So I got a cab there and tried my best but they wanted authority, and when I got back —'

'Stitched up good and proper,' said the policeman, scribbling.

Katherine's face was black as thunder. 'It's all gone,' she said. 'Miss Quinton's journals, the notes we made, the spare inventory, the anonymous letter to Evangeline. The whole lot.'

'They jemmied the lock while young Reg was on your false errand,' said the policeman. 'And they knew what they was after.'

I sank into a chair and covered my face. 'What do we do now?' I whispered.

'I'll put the kettle on,' said Reg. 'It ain't much but — Oh no. I ain't falling for that again.'

The telegraph boy stood in the doorway, open-mouthed. 'The door was open,' he said, when he had recovered himself.

'You've caused enough bother,' said Reg, stalking over and snatching the telegram. He scanned it, then walked towards me, holding it out. 'If it says go to an abandoned warehouse or St Paul's Cathedral or summink, rip it up.'

I ripped it open.

Please come home when you get this STOP Moss here distraught STOP Has had anonymous letter like Evangeline's STOP A

CHAPTER 21
Katherine

Connie looked at me in despair.

'Is there a difficulty, madam?' asked the policeman, his pencil poised over his notebook.

'Let's keep together,' I whispered, giving her a hug, and raised my voice. 'Family business. We must attend to it as soon as possible, but first we must find out what happened here.'

'All our notes, everything...' Connie's voice was little more than an agonised murmur.

I forced a confidence I didn't feel. 'It might not be as bad as we think.'

Where to begin? Panic overwhelmed me and despite the draught coming through the open door I felt hot and clammy. The edges of the room started to go black...

'Here, hold up,' said the police officer.

Connie's arm steadied me. 'Sit down, Katherine,' she said. 'Put your head between your knees . . . or at least, put it as low as you can. Don't swoon on the floor, there's too many splinters.'

Things came back into focus and I felt comforted by her shaky smile. I straightened up.

'If I might trouble you Miss, er Mrs, er...' said the policeman, glancing at what was left of my waistline.

'Our proper names are Mrs Lamont and Mrs King,' said Connie. 'Reg, do you know exactly what's missing?'

The room was an utter mess. Our cupboard and the drawers had been broken into. Files and photographs were scattered across the floor. The index-card box had been likewise breached and cards strewn everywhere. Our typewriter had been pushed sideways and the desks moved, the rug pulled back. Pictures were askew.

'I do.' Reg lifted his briefcase onto the desk and removed a notebook and an envelope. His usual optimism had returned. 'Don't worry, ladies. It won't take long to work out what's what if we check things off together. I mean you can see Miss Q's journals have gone, but I got my list of what should be in the cupboard here, cos I took it home to try and work out a better filing system, and look.' He pulled two stiff pieces of card from the envelope. 'I arranged these; I only just picked them up. I hope you don't mind.'

Behind me the postman arrived with the second post, stepping into the room with a strangled exclamation as I took the cards from Reg. They were mounted photographs of Evangeline's anonymous letter.

'Oh no Reg,' said Connie. 'Definitely not.'

***

Outside the traffic was so busy that even with Tredwell's excellent driving we would crawl along.

'We'd probably be quicker walking,' I said, in despair.

'Not with you in your condition,' said Connie. 'Shall we take the tube? We might have more luck with a cab at Baker Street.'

It had been a long time since we'd gone anywhere by underground together. After some protestation from Tredwell, Connie and I pulled our veils down to protect our faces from soot and hurried to the entrance of the tube, passing billboard posters and shrieking newspaper vendors. Somehow, with my mind in turmoil, I was glad to be with lots of people, though anonymous to all of them bar Connie. There we were, women in black — two of many — squashed against people from every walk of life, neither the richest nor poorest, the oldest nor youngest, nor, in my case, the only expectant mother.

It wasn't possible to talk discreetly. I could feel Connie trembling and suspected I was doing the same. I tried to relax by studying my fellow-passengers and memorising details about them. One woman of medium height in a slightly faded heather-coloured coat was reading *The Gentlewoman* avidly. Something about her profile seemed familiar. Her lobeless ear bore a tiny pearl earring, and a rabbit's foot brooch with an amethyst was pinned to her lapel. Her hat was trimmed in the latest style, but with a slightly lopsided look as if she had done it herself without having learnt the skill. I couldn't see her face properly, simply her forehead with its greying Alexandra fringe and heavy eyebrows. I closed my eyes and forced myself to think of what I needed to.

I had known my cousin Moss all my life. He had been fifteen the year I was born, the year his brother Albert was born and their mother died. He had been away at school then university for most of my childhood, and it was only Albert, and occasionally Douglas, who visited our house to play with me. After university Moss threw himself or was thrown into the lion's den of the social whirl: a rich man's son, albeit one with several younger brothers. Until the last few years, we had lost touch. But since Albert and Connie had married, Moss had become like my elder brother: protective, humouring, indulgent, and a little shy.

I looked at Connie. She was so convinced of her idea. Could I be sure he was innocent on the basis of sentiment? If he were guilty then either he had sent letters to Evangeline and himself, or someone else was accusing them both. If the latter, was the accusation based on knowledge or suspicion? As for Uncle Maurice, the cause of death had been given as stroke. He was, after all, seventy-six and what my father called a trencherman — no food was too rich, no wine too strong. It was hard to think my uncle needed poisoning when he was doing it himself. Unless someone wanted to hasten things. I couldn't believe it. I couldn't.

Connie, I suspected, was just as preoccupied and quietening her mind with what the postman had brought. After reading, she passed it over with a significant look. It was the report from the search we'd requested into the women who might have been Jonah's mother.

Ruthe Hillbeam, Whitechapel, convulsions aged five

Ruth Hilbean, Kensington, heart disease aged seventy
Ruby Hilbeem, Ealing, puerperal fever aged eighteen

The date of the latter's death, 21st May 1848, was from my recollection only a few days after Jonah was born. Spelling mistakes were reasonably common. At least one case might be solved.

I put the report in my bag and returned to my thoughts about Moss. It didn't take long to get to Baker Street and Connie was right; we hailed a cab almost immediately and were at her house in no time.

'Where are the gentlemen?' she asked Nancy as our coats were taken.

'They're in the study, ma'am.'

Albert rose when we entered and embraced Connie. Moss remained seated before the fire, his head in his hands. I sat on the arm of the chair and hugged him.

'Hullo Moss,' I said. I didn't know what else to say.

'Where is it?' asked Connie. Her face was grey with worry and she swallowed as she looked from Albert to Moss.

Moss held out a crumpled piece of paper, the stuck-on letters unpeeling a little.

YouLL HanG foR SurE

'Katherine, Connie — is this exactly the same as Evangeline's?'

'Let's see,' I said, and pulled out of my handbag the photographs Reg had taken of the original.

'Thank goodness for Reg,' said Connie.

'I know,' I said. 'We should raise that young man's salary.'

I laid everything on Albert's desk and we all peered. 'That's an unusual G,' said Albert. He was right; I recognised it.

'It's from *The Gentlewoman*,' I said. 'Did you see that lady reading it on the tube today?'

'No, but you could be right,' said Connie.

'First Evangeline and now me,' groaned Moss. 'Why? And oh, I haven't even said anything to her. I've been afraid to write.' He stared down at the papers.

'Moss,' I said. 'I promised myself I wouldn't interfere, but why haven't you written to her?'

Moss lifted his head and rubbed his face as if trying to scarify it. He didn't answer.

'Is it because of Aunt Charlotte?' I said.

'Mother?' said Albert.

Moss stared at me. 'How did you know?'

'I passed a poster for Mr Shaw's play *Widowers' Houses* earlier. Even though it's about something completely different it made me think of Father and Uncle Maurice. I realised you and I were the same age when our mothers died, and I can remember looking at James just before we married and thinking…'

'What if what happened to my father happens to me, and the person that finally stopped your loneliness leaves you on your own?' Moss's voice was a whisper. 'Wouldn't it be better to stay alone and not risk it?'

'Yes,' I said. 'That's exactly what I felt. But I married James because I wasn't complete without him.' I bit my lip. 'Moss, what would you do for Evangeline?'

'Anything,' he said, and smiled sadly. 'I'd live with her in a hovel if she'd have me. I even went to ask Miss Quinton for her blessing that day when we were all at Hazelgrove. I knew the old bird was fond of Evangeline.'

'Did she give it?' said Connie.

'I never got to ask her,' said Moss. 'She pretty much refused me audience and told me to go back to London with the other dirty beasts. But that's not a reason to kill someone.'

Connie was watching him, her face troubled. She turned her attention to the letters.

'Are you sure the *G* is from *The Gentlewoman*, Katherine?' she said. 'I've never read it.'

I closed my eyes to recall, and gasped.

'What is it?' asked Connie.

'I know her. The woman on the tube train, I mean. She's changed her hair, but I know those ears and I remember that brooch. It was Mary Taplow. *You* may not read it, but *she* does.'

Chapter 22
Connie

'Miss Taplow reads *The Gentlewoman*, and she's in London, and she'd have embroidery scissors.' I looked up to find everyone staring at me. 'The same person sent these letters, I'd swear to it.' I got up and bent over the letter and the photograph. 'Plain white paper. The letters are similar. Small scissors. Neatly done.' I turned to Moss. 'Do you have the envelope it came in?'

Moss felt in his pocket and handed it over. 'I was so shaken by it I didn't think to put the letter back in. I just called a cab and came here. I knew that Albert — and you — would know what to do.'

I scanned the envelope. A Charing Cross postmark. 'And posted from the same place.' I looked down at the letter again. I had been so busy examining the printed letters, the paper, the way it had been put together, that I had barely taken in the message: *YouLL HanG foR SurE.*

'Oh, Moss . . . Moss, I'm so sorry.' I looked up at his

sad, shocked face. 'I must apologise.'

'For what?' Moss didn't seem surprised, just exhausted.

I studied the hearthrug for some time before replying. 'I thought it — I thought it might be you,' I whispered, and every word grazed my throat as I said it.

Moss said nothing at first, but I saw that his blue eyes, so like Albert's, were full of horror. 'But why, Connie?' he choked out at last. 'Why me?'

'You — didn't seem yourself. You were doing odd things. Borrowing books about land. Pushing Albert to invest in risky schemes. And that lunch —'

'Oh, those lunches.' Moss's hand tightened on his handkerchief. 'I love — *loved* Father, but —' He blinked. 'He never wanted me to be who I was. He wanted me to be like him, and I couldn't. Lately I've tried to be what Evangeline wants, I've tried to turn my mind to business, I've tried to learn about managing an estate —' He swallowed as if it hurt him. 'And I've never felt less like myself.'

'Oh, Moss!' Katherine got up and put her arms around him. 'You are a fine man just as you are. You don't *have* to be like Uncle Maurice.'

'I feel as if I do,' he muttered. 'I'm the head of the family now. Supposedly.' His tone was as bitter as strong coffee.

'But you don't have to be Father.' Albert went over to his brother and ruffled his hair, and for once immaculate Moss didn't mind. 'In fact most of us would prefer it if you weren't. He could be — well, he was one of a kind.'

'That he was,' said Moss, and a little smile pushed up

the edges of his moustache. I tried to remember the last time I had seen him smile properly — was it James and Lucy's birthday party? It seemed a lifetime ago.

'Anyway, you can trust me to look after the business side of things,' said Albert. 'Father named me his executor —'

'Another thing he didn't trust me to do —'

'Would you want to do it?' Albert asked.

Moss considered for a moment. 'Um, no.' The smile returned. 'I don't think I would.'

'Thought so.' Albert grinned at him. 'Let's just get ourselves back to normal. Or what passes for it.'

'That sounds like a plan,' I said, softly. I got up and held out a hand to Moss. 'Friends?'

Now Moss looked surprised. 'We never *weren't* friends,' he said, shaking my hand. 'And I'm sorry for when I was — odd, and not thinking straight.'

'I wasn't either,' I said, squeezing his hand. 'I should have trusted you.'

Moss massaged his hand gently when I released it. 'What happens now?' he asked. 'About — this?' He indicated the letter on the desk.

'I wonder what she was trying to do,' said Katherine. 'I mean, it's obvious why she'd send a cruel letter to Evangeline, to try and get her to give up her inheritance. But you —'

'Maybe the same,' I said. 'Evangeline hasn't done what she wanted, so perhaps she thought that putting pressure on you would get you to do the job for her.'

'How — disgusting,' said Moss, wrinkling his nose.

'It is,' said Katherine. 'And we'll deal with her in due course.'

'I'd rather you got her arrested now,' said Moss, frowning.

'I'd love to,' Katherine replied. 'But I'm not sure the police would arrest her, and I have a feeling she's more useful at large.'

'Where does she live?' I asked. 'Is it with her brother?'

'I imagine so,' said Katherine. 'I can ask Margaret when I see her next. We have a cook to interview, remember.'

'So is there anything I should be doing?' asked Moss.

Katherine and I looked at each other. '*Yes*,' we said in unison. 'Write to Evangeline!'

'Never mind that,' he said, rising with an air of purpose which I had never seen before. 'I shall go and see her.'

***

'I suppose we should be grateful that they didn't take everything,' I said, as I straightened another picture.

Katherine snorted from her seat at the desk. 'They were only interested in one case,' she said.

A hard Saturday morning's work had brought the office almost back to its old self — but we were painfully conscious of the missing file and the empty drawer. I paused in my work and sat down on the desk, facing Katherine. 'Yes, but who is "they"?'

'How ungrammatical,' said Katherine. 'But a good question.' She ticked off the points on her fingers. 'Someone who's in London, obviously.'

'Yes. And who knows we're involved with the case and wants us to back off.'

'Indeed. Where's that telegram? If it's Charing Cross —' She opened the drawer of her desk. 'Can you remember where we filed it?'

'Here.' I fished it out of my in-tray. 'It was sent from Holborn.'

'Not far away, then.' Katherine took it from me and read it out. *'Please check Taplow date and place of birth Somerset House URGENT Miss F.'*

'Interesting,' I said. 'Miss Taplow almost certainly didn't send it, because she wouldn't want to draw attention to herself. So who did?'

'Who else is in London?' Katherine stared at me, as if for inspiration. 'Latimer!'

'That would be quick work, though,' I said. 'To figure out who we were and what we were up to.' I sighed. 'There I was, thinking he liked me.'

'Oh do shut up, Connie.' Katherine began counting again. 'So not Taplow, not Latimer. Mrs Booth? She's in London.'

'But why?' I asked. 'She's one of the few people we haven't considered.'

'True.' Katherine pondered. 'I'll ask Margaret to slip in a reference to Holborn or a telegram when she does the interview, and watch for a response.' She sighed, and stroked her stomach.

'Are you all right?' I came to sit on her desk.

'I'm fine.' Katherine smiled up at me, but dark circles showed under her eyes.

'How is James?'

She grimaced. 'Much better in himself, but restless.

Fretting about the paper. Nathan visited the other day and James gave him about fifty things to do at the office.' She yawned. 'He looked as if he had the world on his shoulders when he left.'

'Ah. The burden of responsibility.' I tried not to think of the responsibilities waiting for me at home; meals to order, visits to pay, and letters to answer. One of those letters was from Jemima, enquiring whether I had had leisure to consider the matter she had brought to my attention a short while ago. I winced. 'I should probably be getting home. And you look as if a nap wouldn't go amiss.'

'Perhaps you're right.' Katherine held out a hand and I helped her up. 'I can see how the invalid is getting on. If I know him, he's probably sitting up in bed writing an editorial.'

'Whatever keeps him out of trouble.' I moved round the office double-checking the drawer locks and the window catches. 'Shutting the stable door, but —'

'That reminds me,' said Katherine, pulling a report from her bag. 'Should we keep this here, or shall I take it home?'

'We haven't been able to make a copy, so until we have...' I turned the paper over, and froze. 'This entry, about Ruby Hillbeem...'

'Oh, it'll keep till Monday,' said Katherine, putting on her coat. 'I'm sure Jonah Hillbeam will be glad of the information, but —' Seeing my expression, she came to peer at the paper with me.

'Look. *Informant: Mr P.F. Taplow, of the same address. Employer.*'

We stared at each other and I consulted the sheet of paper again. *The Colonnades, Ealing.*

'Miss Taplow wouldn't have been born,' I said. 'Or she'd have been a child, at most. Maybe we *should* check her place and date of birth.'

'There's a connection, though,' said Katherine, running her finger down the page. 'A maid in trouble. A woman whose family had come down in the world. And Taplow and Hillbeam were both in the house when Miss Quinton died.' She looked up at me and her green eyes were almost black. 'What does it mean?' she whispered.

Chapter 23
Katherine

'Are you sure this is legal?' Connie whispered. 'And are you in a draught? Pull that wrap up.'

We were sitting in a room adjoining Miss Thirza Gregory's drawing room. It was a good thing hers was an old house with secret spyholes, intentional or otherwise. We peeked through the gap where Margaret was sitting tapping her foot. Miss Gregory sat placidly beside her.

'If asked,' I murmured back, 'I can argue that I'm picking up tips for hiring a cook.'

'Are you *finally* going to hire one?' said Connie.

I nodded. 'Of course. We can't manage on sausages and soup once the baby comes. I've made enquiries about a cook and a nursemaid and I've already hired another maid to come after Christmas and help out with all the extra work.'

'Goodness, you never said.' Connie looked at me in surprise as she hugged herself. Miss Gregory was another old lady who didn't approve of unnecessary fires. 'I thought you would try and manage by yourself as usual.'

'I'm sure I don't know why everyone thinks I'm stupid.'

I felt a little out of sorts and wasn't entirely sure why. I had snapped at James that morning and now I was snapping at Connie. My mind and body were not playing fair. Nausea had been replaced by appetite, and appetite by moods which ranged from reckless to miserable. I was even managing to aggravate myself. As for the baby, it must be sleepy today as I could not recall a solitary kick. Was that normal? I didn't dare ask.

'No-one thinks you're stupid,' Connie said, looking rather hurt. 'However, you do tend towards excessive independence. Are you feeling all right?'

'I wish everyone would stop fussing. I —'

'Shh, here she is.'

From our vantage point we could see Mrs Booth's face as she was shown in by the parlourmaid, but could see neither Margaret's nor Miss Gregory's.

'Ah, thank you Pritchard. Good morning, Mrs Booth,' said Miss Gregory. 'Do take a seat. Would you like coffee or tea?'

'Tea please, ma'am,' said Mrs Booth. 'I find coffee interferes with the tastebuds.'

'Very well. Tea please, Pritchard.' Miss Gregory settled herself more comfortably in her chair.

'It's a pleasure to meet you Mrs Demeray, Miss Demeray,' said Mrs Booth.

Miss Gregory gave a small giggle which she turned into a cough. 'Well now Mrs Booth, I'm simply here to guide my daughter. She will ask the questions.'

'Good morning, Mrs Booth,' said Margaret. 'I am, as you know, intending to marry in a few months time and I need a cook.'

'They'll be living here, of course,' interrupted Miss Gregory. 'Since otherwise I'll be all on my own. One day,' she sniffed and dabbed her eyes, 'it'll be theirs.'

I could just make out Mrs Booth's eyes taking in the well-appointed room and the silk of the two black-clad ladies before her.

'Don't you have a cook already, ma'am?'

'She's retiring,' said Margaret, regaining her nerve, 'and in any event, my darling Alexander and I shall be entertaining a great deal.'

'Who's Alexander?' whispered Connie.

'No idea. Hopefully someone from a book.'

'What kind of entertaining, Miss Demeray, if I may ask?' said Mrs Booth.

'Lavish,' drawled Margaret. 'Have you heard of Escoffier?'

Mrs Booth visibly bridled. 'A cook is very much preferable to a mere chef. I can produce not only the finest French cuisine but also a good English roast and the most delicate cakes. Escoffier, indeed! Everyone so excited about pêche Melba last year, when *anyone* can plonk a peach on a plate with ice-cream and jam.' She took a breath as Pritchard returned with the tea, and puffed up with patriotic pride. 'An English cook is worth ten French cooks from the Savoy.'

'So there,' whispered Connie.

I stuffed my wrap in my mouth to smother my giggles and hoped the slight rumble in my stomach wasn't audible.

'Er, indeed,' said Margaret. 'Could you tell us a little about your previous employment?'

Mrs Booth sipped her tea and calmed a little. 'Yes of course, Miss. I started as a tweeny in London in 1861, a gent's house in Lincoln's Inn. I worked up to kitchen maid, and on the day the cook was sick and I was allowed to do the dessert, one of the guests recognised my talent. In 1873 I took over the kitchens at Athelrampton House and stayed five years. I'm sure you've heard how particular her Ladyship is.'

'If one is paying for the best, one expects the best,' said Miss Gregory. 'Although don't you mean Abinhampton House? I presume you refer to the Dowager Lady Athalea.'

Mrs Booth licked her lips. 'Yes ma'am, of course. It was a long time ago. I got muddled.'

'Oh!' exclaimed Margaret, perusing a document in her lap. 'I see you had a restaurant of your own in Gerrard Street.'

'Yes, Miss,' said Mrs Booth, casting a glare at the document that threatened to ignite it. 'Sad to say I couldn't continue for long.'

'And that was when you moved to Lion House.'

'Yes, Miss. 1879, that was. It's a fine house, and Miss Quinton could afford the richest food, but she rarely entertained.'

'And yet you stayed,' said Miss Gregory.

Mrs Booth sounded a little truculent. 'Miss Quinton remembered me in her will, you know. That proves how much she thought of me. Poor blessed kind old lady.'

'That's the first time I've heard her described that way,' whispered Connie.

'Now let me see,' said Margaret as if pondering what to say next. 'How do you work with other servants?'

Mrs Booth's mouth narrowed into a sardonic smile for one second before pursing.

'As long as everyone knows their place, Miss, all is well,' she said. 'What we had to endure at Lion House. Finicking. Fine food spurned for slops on account of a figure. And her forty if she's a day. As if *he'd* notice.'

'Which servant was that?' said Thirza in surprise. 'I wonder she wasn't dismissed.'

'Not a servant exactly. The companion. She wearied him and poor Miss Quinton no end with her endless sucking up.' Mrs Booth put on refined tones. '"If only Father hedn't been *so* confused about money, I'd be mistress of our *fine* home." Fine home my . . . Aunt Norah. She showed me a daguerreotype once and it was just some rotten-looking pile with *Colonnades, Ealing* written across the corner. "Now my brother has to earn a living like a *common man* and live in a *flet* orf the Strend," she'd say.'

'The Strand is such a mixed sort of place,' interrupted Margaret casually. 'Lincoln's Inn, Holborn, Charing Cross . . . they have changed such a lot. Do you know Holborn at all, Mrs Booth? I understand it's much improved.'

Mrs Booth grinned. 'I'm sure her brother isn't in as fancy a bit of the Strand as she'd like us to believe, but it didn't stop her. I'm sorry Miss, but she riled the servants something rotten. Made them cry, especially poor old Hillbeam — that was the parlourmaid. Miss Quinton didn't reward the companion with much, but she'd only been with us a couple of years.'

'Can you give me an example of the menus?' said Margaret.

'Not a great many. As I say, Miss Quinton kept a quiet house. Ladies for tea. Sometimes a Mr Latimer visited. He's an art dealer, rather persistent. The companion was the only one keen on him. "Of course he taught me *everything* about art!" she'd say. He liked his food, though, and maybe he could give me a reference.'

'Do you have his address?'

Mrs Booth licked her lips again and pondered the ceiling. 'He has a gallery in Brompton, Miss.'

'Thank you, Mrs Booth,' said Margaret. 'We'll be in touch through the agency.'

Pritchard detached herself from the wall and escorted the cook out. We waited in the study as Margaret and Miss Gregory sat chatting companionably about nothing until the front door shut with a definite bang.

'Fresh tea and cups, ma'am?' said Pritchard, putting her head round the door.

'Yes please, Pritchard,' said Miss Gregory. 'Come in, girls,' she called.

'Did you notice what Mrs Booth said?' Connie ran her finger down her notes. 'She reported Mary Taplow as saying "He taught me everything about art". That suggests she knew Mr Latimer before she was at Lion House.' She turned to Miss Gregory. 'I don't suppose you want to advertise for a companion?'

'I think not, dear,' said Miss Gregory. 'This investigating is too exhausting. I daresay Miss Taplow will be advertising herself in *The Lady*. That's the usual place, isn't it?'

'That's true,' said Connie. Her face had fallen a little and mine had too. Miss Gregory hadn't said a truer word. Exhausting.

'Thanks, Margaret,' I said, embracing my sister.

'What a palaver,' she answered, with a small kiss. 'I think I'll stick to a *flet orf the Strend* and do my own cooking. If any rich Americans want entertaining I'll take them to the Savoy.'

'With Alexander?'

'Maybe.' Her eyes went misty. Then she looked at me more closely. 'What's wrong, Kitty? Something is.'

'Nothing,' I said.

Pritchard returned with the tea and a letter which she waved at Miss Gregory. 'I'm so sorry ma'am, I couldn't find a stamp and it's missed the post. I've found one now but it may not get there tomorrow.'

Margaret spluttered and nudged me. The envelope was emitting a soft scent of violets and was written in purple ink. *R Demeray Esq, Hazelgrove…*

'Oh dear,' said Miss Gregory, catching our expressions. 'Perhaps I should explain.'

***

'Who first?' said Connie in the cab.

'I can't think about Miss Gregory sending perfumed letters to Father,' I answered. 'Margaret can ask those questions. We'll have to see what Reg has found out, although it sounds as if there's some sort of link.'

'I meant you and me.'

'You and me?'

'Let me start. My family — my sisters — are being an utter nuisance.'

'Veronica?'

'Now it's Jemima. She has given me a conundrum and she won't let me ask you to help.'

'But you're telling me anyway.'

'I have to. I feel like I'm going to explode,' said Connie. 'And you hate me for suspecting Moss.' A tear ran down her cheek.

'Oh, Connie.' I squeezed her hand. 'You had to be the voice of doubt to clear him. I could never hate you.'

'As long as you're sure.'

We sat in silence for a while. For once the day was fine, the sun watery but bright in the sky. 'Connie, may I ask you something?'

'Of course.'

'Did your babies kick every day?'

Connie wiped the tear away. 'Oh, Katherine. Is that what's been bothering you? No, they didn't. Some days they didn't move at all. Maybe your baby is as tired as you look. You must rest more.'

'Not many women have the luxury to rest,' I said.

'No, they don't,' said Connie, 'but they should. That's the difference. And if you're worried, ask the doctor. At least you can afford to do that. For now, just talk to it.'

'Him.'

'Do you think so?'

'Yes. I don't know why. But yes. Anyway, I shall, I promise. Where were we?'

'Pulling ourselves together,' said Connie. 'Goodness, the Embankment. Do you remember when...'

Both of us went quiet, remembering our first case. Somehow almost all of my recollection involved kissing. I tried not to giggle.

'I've no idea how, but that's cheered you up.' Connie smiled.

We joined Reg at the office. 'Here you go, ladies,' said Reg. 'It's taken me all morning and it's awful.' He took out his notebook.

'A Dr McNess signed Ruby Hilbeem's death certificate. She was a maid of all work at The Colonnades in Ealing, wherever that was. It's not there now. There's a road called The Colonnades but it's all villas. She died of puerperal fever.'

Connie and I exchanged glances.

'Thing is, I tracked down Dr McNess. He's still there. Took over the practice about thirty years ago. He was newly qualified in 1848, just a young 'un. So cheap. He's getting on a bit, but he's never forgotten it. His first certificate of death, he said. His face went red then grey when I asked him. "They're gone now," he said, "so it doesn't matter. Dash the Hippocratic oath," he said, "I've wanted to tell someone for years."'

'Dash?' said Connie.

'You're a lady,' said Reg. 'Not like some who said they were.'

'Go on,' I said.

'An old woman lived there, he said, with a son called Peter and a new daughter-in-law. The house was big but full of rot and worm. Amazing none of them had pneumonia or consumption, he said. As for the maids, they kept leaving. Bad wages, worse conditions. They had a cook and two maids when the death certificate was written. Ruth and Ruby, but Ruby was really a Ruth too. Employers change servants' names, don't they? Like they don't matter.'

'What did they do when she died?' asked Connie.

'He said they didn't care,' said Reg. 'Didn't care enough to remember her real first name, didn't care enough to wonder where her baby was. They just wanted her body off the premises as fast as you like. They asked him to send his bill in, and he heard them whisper, "If it's too much, we'll ask Adeline Latimer." He says he's never got the taste of it out of his mouth.'

CHAPTER 24
Connie

'So the Taplows knew someone called Adeline Latimer,' Katherine said slowly. 'Would anyone mind if I sat down?'

'It can't be a coincidence,' I said.

'Latimer as in that chap you asked me to shadow?' Reg put his elbows on the desk.

'The very same,' I replied. 'What did you manage to find out?'

Reg wrinkled his nose. 'Precious little. He goes out to do his business, his business doesn't come to him — so I can't tell you about any visitors. And when he does go out he takes a cab, not a train or a tube. He goes to his club of an evening when he goes out at all. He stays up till midnight most nights, and he writes a lot of letters.'

'And we know through Mrs Booth that he's a persistent art dealer…'

'Twenty minutes in his shop would tell you that,' said Katherine, nudging me.

'Also that Taplow knew him before . . . he had "taught" her.'

'I'll bet he had,' said Katherine, grimly.

'Oh, don't.' I stifled a grin at the thought of poor dull Miss Taplow hanging on Mr Latimer's every word. 'Anyway, he was known at the house, and he must have been accepted there, to visit at Christmas... Now, what might have happened to make Miss Quinton want to change her will on Christmas Day?'

'My head is spinning,' said Katherine, holding on to the arm of her chair.

'So is mine,' I said. 'If only we still had the journals.'

'If only...' Katherine gazed into the distance.

'You look as if you're miles away,' I said. 'Back to the present with you.'

'I was miles away.' Katherine's gaze focused. 'Just like Miss Quinton.'

I gawped at her. 'I beg your pardon?'

'She travelled, didn't she? To Italy, among other places. And she said that she needed to find — what was it? A safe place for her *souvenir*.'

'She probably brought back all sorts of things,' I said. 'Look at the amount of stuff she had at Lion House.'

'This was a special souvenir,' said Katherine, and her eyes glinted like emeralds. 'A remembrance of an event which happened while she was abroad.' She grinned at me. 'Connie, how old would you say Mr Latimer was, roughly?'

'*Oh!*' I pictured sleek, dark, not-entirely-English Mr Latimer, smiling as he pressed my fingers over his card.

'Mid-thirties? Perhaps early forties?'

'That sounds about right.' Katherine frowned. 'Yet he witnessed the will, and wasn't left anything.'

'Because Miss Quinton wouldn't recognise him as her son,' I said. 'She gave him things from the house to support him — and perhaps to keep him quiet, too.'

'And he witnessed a will which reduced Taplow's inheritance in favour of Evangeline, who only knew Miss Quinton as an old lady.'

'Not just Evangeline, though.' I remembered Mr Strutt's office in the sky, and bending over the will. 'Hillbeam got an annuity, and she paid for Tessie to go to school.'

'Do you know,' Katherine said thoughtfully, 'I thought they might be working together, since there had been a Hillbeam at Taplow's house, and she knew Latimer before.'

'It's like one of them farces,' said Reg. 'You know, where everyone's trying to get something done and they all work against each other, and everyone falls flat on their face.'

I beamed at Reg. 'Young man,' I said, 'you're a born detective.'

Reg bowed. 'It is, though,' he said. 'It's ridikerlus.'

'I'm inclined to agree with you, Reg,' I replied. 'In honour of our breakthrough, I propose lunch at Simpson's. After which, we can continue this conversation. Overtime rates for you, Reg, of course.'

***

'I could just fall asleep now,' said Katherine, settling herself comfortably in her chair.

'Oh no you don't,' I said. 'We've got a case on the brink of being solved. No sleep for you, Miss Caster.'

'Humph.' Katherine pulled herself upright. 'Put the kettle on, Reg, and make it a strong one.'

'Right you are, Miss C.' Reg took some time getting up. He had eaten his considerable fill at Simpson's, marvelling all the while at the joints of meat, the heaps of mashed potatoes, the enormous puddings. 'Oof.'

'I always find I think better after a good lunch,' I said. Katherine and Reg both groaned. 'Now, Taplow. Miss Quinton changed her will and reduced her legacy while Latimer was there. Connected?'

'Almost certainly,' said Katherine. 'Yet if Taplow had done something to annoy Miss Quinton, why didn't she just dismiss her? And why did she raise Hillbeam's legacy, and Tessie's? She could have kept them the same.'

'She could. Come along, kettle.' I picked up the post, which Reg had brought up with him. I recognised Jemima's handwriting on the first letter, and hastily put it to the back.

'What's that?' asked Katherine, sharply.

'I thought you were asleep,' I retorted. 'Nothing to worry about. Personal letter.'

'To the office?' Katherine raised her eyebrows.

'Why don't you help Reg make the tea?' Katherine rolled her eyes, but complied. I put the rest of the letters down, took up my letter-opener, and broke the seal.

Connie, please either say you'll do it or no. I can't sleep for worrying. J.

I laid the letter gently on the desk and sighed.

'Should I ask?' called Katherine.

'Please don't.' I put my elbows on the desk, my chin on my hands, and stared at Jemima's scrawl. I wanted to make her feel better; of course I did.

But what if I made her feel much, much worse?

'Tea,' said Katherine, putting the cup well away from both my elbows and the letter. 'Is that from Jemima? You look as if she's invited you to scrub her floors and remove the spiders from her cellar.'

'I wish she had,' I replied, still staring at the letter.

'So say no.' Katherine patted my shoulder and returned to her chair with her own cup.

'Sometimes, you know, you talk a lot of sense.'

Katherine grinned. 'One tries.'

I hunted in the drawer for plain notepaper. 'Only sometimes, mind you. Let me deal with this, and I'll get back to the case in hand.'

'Fair enough.' Katherine sipped her tea. 'Why don't you hand me the rest of the mail, and I'll go through it while you write your letter.'

I did as I was told, then sat and resisted the urge to chew the end of my pen.

Dear Jemima,
Please excuse the delay in my response.

It was a beginning, at any rate.

I am afraid I cannot carry out the task you request. You

are my sister; but Charles is my friend. If you have concerns, my advice is that you talk to him, and come at the truth that way.

I do not believe that the course of action which you suggested will help. At best, it will confirm your suspicions. At worst, it could lead to an unhealable rift.

If you wish to discuss this further, please come and see me at home.

Sincerely,
Connie

I blotted the missive, found and addressed an envelope, and slipped the note inside. 'Better?' asked Katherine.

'Better.' I smiled. 'Reg, would you mind running this to the post office? You can catch the next post if you hurry.'

Reg gave me a pained look, but took the letter with good grace. 'I might take it steady on the way back, if you don't mind,' he said, as he closed the door.

'Sorry about that,' I said. 'It had to be done, though. I've spent enough time sorting out Veronica, without adding Jemima to the list. I can't solve all their problems.'

'Well, we can sort out Jonah Hillbeam, at any rate,' said Katherine. 'I'm sure this is his writing.' She held up a thick cream-coloured envelope, addressed in a hand with many loops and flourishes.

I frowned. 'I still haven't written to him about Ruth,' I said. 'Although perhaps that's a good thing, now Reg has found out so much more. Come on, let's see what he says.' I passed her the letter opener.

'*Dear Misses Castor and Fleet,*' Katherine read. 'Oh

bless the man, he's spelt me like castor oil.'

'Do be quiet,' I said. 'Or rather, don't.'

'*I am writing to thank you for your kind efforts in finding my family. My aunt and uncle Hillbeam — I smile as I say their names — have been staying with me since you reunited us. I couldn't let them stay in some down-at-heel temperance hotel. We have been talking nineteen to the dozen about old times, for we have much to catch up on.*

I put them on the train today, but I have invited them to spend Christmas with us, and in the interim I intend to make provision for them in my will. It's shameful that they have had to work so long, and I have let them know they will never have to depend on charity if I can help it.

Don't forget to send in your bill as I am well able to manage it. I am indebted to you in more ways than one.

Yours with thanks,

J Hillbeam Esq'

'That's a nice letter,' I said. 'I really must write with our news.'

Katherine said nothing.

'You can write if you'd rather,' I said. 'I don't mind.' Then I looked at her properly. 'What on earth is it?'

'There's another letter, from Inspector Havelock. The vintners replied to his enquiry.' Katherine looked up from the sheet. 'The bottle of port which poisoned James was from a very small batch. The warehouse at Douro deal only with that vintner in this country. Half the batch went to the Queen, for entertaining, and Miss Quinton took the remainder for Lion House.'

Reg opened the door, panting slightly. 'All done,' he said. 'Got it in the post.' Then he saw our faces. 'Don't tell me you want me to take another letter.'

'Worse than that, Reg,' I said. 'Run and hold a cab for us. Before anyone else dies.'

Chapter 25
Katherine

'Can you print them today?' I said. 'I wouldn't ask, but we think there are lives at stake. *A* life at least.'

Mr Harper looked round his print room and sucked his teeth.

'Well, we've got a run of counterfeit fivers drying out, but…' He gave me a grin. 'Just joking. Course I can, love. Anything for my favourite niece-in-law or whatever you are.' He perused the paper I'd handed him. 'Cor blimey, but your writing is shocking.'

'It always is when she panics,' said Connie.

'I wasn't panicking. It was bouncy in the carriage,' I said with dignity. 'How long do you need, Mr Harper?'

'For you, love, half an hour. That do you?'

'Perfect; that gives us time to make a call to Mr Strutt from Penelope's,' said Connie. 'I'm sure she won't mind.'

'Has Mr Strutt a telephone?' Given the way Connie had described the solicitor's office, it seemed unlikely.

'Oh yes,' Connie confirmed, before instructing Tredwell to head to James's aunt's house. 'I took the number in case it was necessary. I suppose London clients nowadays often have a telephone. At least it stops people having to clamber all the way up to his lair for a simple question.'

'You sure you want me to send this telegram to Miss King?' said Reg, hanging on to the side of the carriage and looking faintly sick. 'I didn't oughta have eaten that extra Yorkshire pudding.'

'Yes, Reg,' I said. 'She'll understand. We'll drop you at the telegraph office as we pass and pick you up shortly.'

James's aunt Penelope was her usual calm self, quite unconcerned when Connie and I rapped at her door and requested the use of her telephone. Without any questions, she led us to the instrument and offered us tea.

'No time,' I said. 'But thank you.'

'Would you like me to climb out of cabs in disguise?' she said. 'Or dangle by one slipping hand off the new Tower Bridge?'

'Not today, I'm afraid,' I confessed.

'Next time, perhaps,' she said, settling in an armchair with a cigarette to watch us. Connie began the call, while I flicked through a copy of *Debrett's* which must have dated from Aunt Penelope's youth.

'Hullo, Mr Strutt,' bellowed Connie, after the usual period of connection through the exchange and the answering yell at the other end. 'Might you tell me Miss Taplow's correspondence address? I believe she wanted to be notified should Miss King wish to contact her. Which she does. Ah good, I thought so... Yes of course I'll wait...' She rolled her eyes at me. I could almost hear the rummaging at the other end, and then Connie started to write in her notebook. 'Thank you, Mr Strutt, thank you. Goodbye.'

'Thank you, Aunt Penelope,' I said, giving her a quick kiss as we rushed out. 'When we require anyone to hang by a thread over the Thames, I'll know where to come.'

'A pleasure,' she said, waving us goodbye.

We picked up Reg and asked Tredwell to rush back to the printers.

'Did that old *Debrett's* help at all?' asked Connie, as the carriage bowled along.

'It did!' I read from my notes. 'LATIMER, *Augustus* Mortimer Randolph, born 1776, m. Edwina Raine Victoria, daughter of the late Edward Quinton. Sons living: two. Daughters living: Adeline Augusta Victoria, born February 1811, of Salix House, Finchley. Issue: Adoptive son, born 1851.'

'1851,' said Connie. 'So that son would be in his early forties today.'

'Miss Quinton begins to mention Mr Latimer — "A" — in 1887. Adeline would have been in her seventies. I'm guessing she died that year.' I swallowed and counted on my fingers. 'I'm sure the journal entry about the souvenir was May 1851. If so, she was four months pregnant. And Adeline was a sort of cousin...'

'Who was willing to adopt a souvenir Miss Quinton didn't want...'

'And then couldn't visit her — Miss Quinton said it was impossible for her to come. Now we know why.'

I stroked my stomach surreptitiously. I couldn't imagine for one moment giving my baby away, and if for some reason I had to, I couldn't imagine not longing for his return.

As promised, Mr Harper had the invitations ready when we returned. There were seven in total.

'Are you sure about this one?' I said.

'Yes,' said Connie. 'Think of the port.'

I pondered for a moment. 'Oh goodness, you're right.'

She took a fountain pen from her bag and started to inscribe the envelopes in neat, anonymous script. 'I shall address these since your handwriting is affected by the jolting. We do need the post office to be able to direct the out-of-town ones.' She bit the end of her pen and frowned. 'Why don't we post the local ones, too?'

'I want to see their faces when they open them,' I said. 'I think it will help us.'

We put four in a post-box and as the carriage rattled towards the Strand I pulled out the other papers we had: the ones which had never been filed, the notes we'd made from memory.

'Poor Ruth Hillbeam found herself pregnant just a few years before Miss Quinton. She so wanted her souvenir, yet didn't live to keep it.'

'Why didn't she *tell* me?' said Connie. '*Why* didn't she tell me?'

'I beg your pardon?'

'No, that's not how Keziah Hillbeam said it,' Connie shook her head. 'She said, "Why didn't she tell *me?*"'

I closed my eyes, trying to recall, and when I opened

them saw Miss Taplow on the pavement. 'Stop the carriage, Reg,' I said. 'I'm not sure it's safe for me to lean out of the window.'

As we pulled to a stop I opened the door and alighted, dashing under an awning. 'Good afternoon, Miss Taplow,' I said.

Mary Taplow started. She was still wearing the heather-coloured coat and carried a small brown-paper package tied in string. Steady rain was pouring off the edges of her umbrella. Her eyes were hollow, her mouth turned down more than ever. She regarded me and the carriage with Connie and Reg inside before straightening her back and looking down her nose at me as usual. 'Good afternoon, Mrs King. May I offer my condolences at the loss of your uncle.'

'Thank you,' I said. 'I was about to pay you a visit.'

Mary Taplow's glance flicked towards the side-street which I knew led to the flat where she lived with Frank. Mrs Booth was right. While respectable, it was not likely to be as fancy as Mary Taplow had made out. 'I can't think why,' she said. 'Unless to *insinuate* that my brother is not good enough for your sister.'

'I'm sure he's quite good enough for anyone, Miss Taplow,' I answered. 'I simply wished to deliver this.' I held out one of the envelopes. After a second's hesitation, despite the umbrella, she managed to open it with trembling fingers. She half-smiled.

'Thank you, Mrs King. I presume you are aware of the contents, and it's not before time. I imagine you will shortly be spending time at Lion House. It was like home to me, and I miss it so. Thank you again. Good-day.' She bowed.

'Speaking of Lion House, I saw Hillbeam in London the other day. Did you?' I said.

Mary Taplow looked askance. 'I did not,' she said. 'Although in any case I don't take notice of servants in the street.'

'An unusual name, Hillbeam.'

'I associate it with lack of consideration. My grandmother was always very scathing about a skivvy she had before I was born, called Hillbeam or some such name. The wretch caused no end of bother. As a little girl, if ever I was difficult or caused a fuss, she'd say, "You're a useless, idle troublemaker of a Hillbeam."'

'Troublemaker?'

Mary Taplow flushed. 'She used another word which I won't repeat. The girl had had a baby and, being unmarried, presumably abandoned it.'

'I'm sure you'd never use such a word yourself, even to a servant. No matter how disrespectful they were.'

'I hope I know how to behave, Mrs King,' said Mary Taplow, tucking the envelope into her bag. 'Thank you for the letter. Otherwise, as I say, I do not think your sister is suitable for Frank and I doubt we need meet again.' She marched off into the rain without a backward glance.

The Monsarrat Agency directed us to a restaurant in Pimlico. 'Being under-cook is just a temporary measure,' said Mrs Booth. 'I'm waiting to hear about a permanency.' She looked me over and frowned. 'Have you a relation getting married shortly?'

'I hope not,' I said, and handed her an envelope. She dusted off her hands and opened it. There was no disguising the glint in her eyes.

'Interesting,' she said. 'And only right. All that messing about in my kitchen. Good-day Mrs King. Thanks for this. Things are looking up.'

Augustus Latimer rubbed his hands together when he saw the carriage pull up outside the shop. He brightened at the sight of Connie when we entered and shook her hand warmly. 'Made your choice?' he murmured. 'A nymph? An Etruscan horse? Or perhaps both.'

'Actually,' said Connie. 'I have something for you.'

Mr Latimer took the envelope with a satisfied smirk. 'How kind,' he said, and bowed.

'I'm merely undertaking a favour for a dear friend,' said Connie.

'Indeed?' Mr Latimer broke the seal with a long fingernail and pulled out the contents. His eyebrows rose, but his smirk deepened. 'How the universe smiles,' he said, and patted a statue of a lion on the head. 'Did you wish to make a purchase today?'

'Today I am merely a messenger,' said Connie.

'Very good.' Mr Latimer ushered us towards the door. 'The next time, I hope. Now I trust you don't mind if I shut up the shop? I have unexpected arrangements to make.'

Having dropped Reg at home, Tredwell brought me back to Joyce Square before taking Connie to Marylebone. It was nearly six when I walked into James's arms.

'Wherever have you been?' he said. 'I couldn't make head nor tail of your telegram and I've had an even more confusing one from Evangeline. Come and sit down, you look exhausted.'

'I haven't time to sit down,' I said, as he held me tight. 'We have to pack. We must go to Hazelgrove tomorrow.'

The baby inside me jerked awake and gave a kick so hard that even James felt it.

'There you go,' he said. 'That's two of us telling you to sit down. I'm sure Ada will do a better job anyway. Hazelgrove, eh? Whatever are you up to?'

I handed him the handwritten instruction I'd given to Mr Harper.

Miss Evangeline King cordially invites you to discuss alternative provisions from Miss Henrietta Quinton's will at Lion House, Hazeldown, at eleven o'clock on Monday 26th November.

CHAPTER 26
Connie

Evangeline jumped as the doorbell rang. 'That will be Mr Latimer,' she muttered. 'Everyone else is here already.'

She made to get up but Katherine motioned to her to sit. 'Let them wait. The invitation said eleven o'clock, and it's barely ten minutes to.'

'Yes, but —'

'But nothing. Everything is under control. You don't have to worry about a thing. Does she, Moss?'

Moss, who was sitting beside Evangeline on the sofa, shook his head. 'Just let Caster and Fleet handle it,' he said, smiling at her and taking her hand.

'Oh, there is *one* thing you should do, Evangeline,' I said.

'What?' said Evangeline, looking apprehensive.

I mimed putting a chain inside the neckline of my dress. 'Oh!' she exclaimed, and hid the ring away with a shy smile.

***

Seven chairs, set in a semicircle in the parlour of Lion House, and seven occupants.

Mr Latimer sat on the left, with Miss Taplow next to him. I noted from my vantage point in the hall that her chair had moved a little closer to his, and a little further from the other five chairs. Next to her sat Mrs Booth, looking straight ahead, with her arms folded. Jimmy Hillbeam sat in the centre chair, holding his cap, and his sister's chair was close. Sukey, again, sat a little apart, and Tessie, wearing a very smart dress, was sitting in the right-hand chair, feet together and hands in her lap.

Evangeline cleared her throat. 'Thank you for coming today. I know some of you have had to travel, and I appreciate you taking the trouble.'

Various murmurs and rustlings came from the semicircle of chairs, and a warm, sympathetic smile from Mr Latimer.

'I am aware that you were perhaps — surprised by Miss Quinton's will…'

Miss Taplow puffed up with indignation, while Hillbeam and Tessie beamed and Sukey smirked.

'Therefore I have sought advice on the matter.' That was our cue. I stepped back to let Mr Strutt enter first, then Katherine. I followed her, and Inspector Havelock brought up the rear. The two men placed chairs for us, and we sat facing the semicircle. Miss Taplow glared at us, while Latimer raised an eyebrow, and the Hillbeams joined hands.

'Mr Strutt, if you would be so kind,' said Evangeline,

rather quickly.

Mr Strutt coughed. 'Thank you, Miss King.' He surveyed the semicircle. 'As you know, Miss King, as the residuary legatee, inherited the majority of Miss Quinton's estate.'

'Get on with it,' muttered Sukey, just loud enough to be heard.

'However all of you, with the exception of Mr, ah, Latimer and Mr Hillbeam, received a bequest. Mr Hillbeam was of very recent employ, and as a witness to the will, Mr Latimer of course knew that he was not a beneficiary.'

Sukey sighed.

'I have received notice of a challenge to Miss Quinton's last will and testament, brought by Miss Taplow.' He regarded her thoughtfully.

'Yes,' said Miss Taplow. 'I maintain that my mistress was under undue influence when she changed her will.' She stared at Evangeline, who gazed calmly back at her.

'Mmm. It is fortunate that, as yet, no monies have been paid out, other than those required to run the house.'

I gave Evangeline a tiny nudge, and she started. 'Oh yes. In an effort to determine the truth of the matter, I engaged an agency to assist me. The Caster and Fleet Agency.'

'Shall we?' Katherine said, and we rose to our feet. 'Several of you know me as Mrs King, but Miss Caster is my professional name.'

'And I answer to Miss Fleet at work,' I added. I noted that Mr Latimer's sympathetic smile was quite gone.

'We have devoted much time to our study of the case,'

said Katherine. 'We have also discussed elements of it with Inspector Havelock.'

All eyes turned to the Inspector, sitting composed and silent in his chair. Sukey wriggled.

Katherine continued. 'As you know there was some concern that Miss Quinton's death was not entirely natural —'

'Rubbish,' snapped Miss Taplow. 'She was eighty if she was a day, and ill to boot.'

'In that case, let me put your mind at rest,' I said. 'Miss Quinton was not murdered by any one of the people in this room.'

A collective sigh. I let the silence hang in the air.

'However, certain irregularities in the case complicated our investigation no end.' I smiled at Katherine. 'Miss Caster, perhaps you would like to begin.'

'The first complication,' said Katherine, 'was disappearing fish knives.'

'What?' exclaimed Mr Latimer.

'Apostle spoons were also a matter of conjecture.' Katherine grinned. 'It quickly became clear that someone was making away with items from the estate. When we checked the inventory against the contents of the house, as Miss King had asked us to do, we found — or rather, did *not* find — items missing ranging from cutlery to sculpture. Some of the sculptures were extremely valuable, and naturally we were concerned.'

'She let me have them!' cried Latimer.

'We shall begin with the small items,' said Katherine. 'Early this morning we visited the fancy-goods shop of a certain Abraham Bass, where we bought some very familiar fish knives, and scented pillows with lace edging and embroidery.' She eyed Sukey. 'I believe that Mr Bass is your fiancé.'

Sukey swallowed, and said nothing.

'Inspector Havelock will deal with you later,' said Katherine. 'Please remain seated.'

'Now back to the more valuable items.' Katherine turned to Latimer. 'Miss Quinton gave them to you, you say.'

Latimer's gaze did not waver. 'Yes, she did.'

'Why?'

One corner of his mouth quirked up. 'I came to this house several times at Miss Quinton's invitation, and I am known here. I even witnessed her will.'

'Indeed,' said Katherine. 'So you knew that she was worth much more to you alive than dead. Particularly as you are her son.'

The room gasped — except for Miss Taplow, whose eyes glittered.

'She wanted to keep that small matter quiet — wanted to keep *you* quiet — and I suspect at least half the stock in your gallery is the result of blackmail.' Katherine paused. 'There were also some letters which upset Miss Quinton.'

'The ones I hid with the cutlery?' Hillbeam's eyes were so wide I could see the whites.

'That's right. Letters written in a foreign hand, which hinted that someone else knew of the existence of a son.' Katherine looked very hard at Mr Latimer, who refused to meet her eyes. 'Unfortunately the whereabouts of the surviving letters is not known, since our office was burgled on Friday and all the items in the case file were stolen.'

The expressions in front of us mingled an attempt at polite inquiry with obvious relief.

'Our office manager was diverted with a telegram to get him out of the way, and then the door was forced with a jemmy,' I said. 'The perpetrator was clearly someone with an interest in the case — so one of you seven — who was in London at the time. That could be Miss Taplow, Mrs Booth, or Mr and Miss Hillbeam, who were visiting a relative.'

'As if I would break a door open!' cried Miss Taplow, with an expression of utter distaste.

'Don't worry, Miss Taplow,' said Katherine. 'You were mentioned in the telegram, so we assumed it wasn't you.'

Miss Taplow relaxed slightly. 'I should think not,' she said, crossing her ankles.

'In any case,' I said, 'we retained copies of several items, including the Lion House inventory and an anonymous letter sent to Miss King.'

'A letter which accused me of murdering Miss Quinton,' said Evangeline, heatedly.

'Yes. A letter intended to hurt, and perhaps to induce Miss King to give up her inheritance to avoid further accusation.' I paused. 'A letter addressed left-handed, in case Miss King had seen the person's writing. A letter made of letters, cut from papers and magazines using embroidery scissors. Periodicals including the *London Evening Standard* and the *Illustrated London News*.'

Miss Taplow was studying the floor as if her life

depended on it.

'It would be interesting to see if the person who sent an anonymous letter to my brother-in-law, also posted from Charing Cross, read the same periodicals,' I said. 'If they did, they might be in more trouble. Mightn't they, Inspector?'

Inspector Havelock nodded. 'It's a distinct possibility, Miss Fleet.'

'Anyway,' I gazed at the row of uncomfortable faces, 'I expect you want me to get to the murder —'

A volley of gasps and squeals shot back at me. Mr Latimer recovered himself first. 'You said no one murdered her!' He looked as if I had cheated him.

'I *almost* said that,' I replied. 'My words were that Miss Quinton was not murdered by any *one* of the people in this room. That is because, from our findings, the evidence points to *many*.'

Jimmy Hillbeam stood up. 'I'm not sitting here to be accused by a pack of women,' he said. 'You've got no right to keep me here.'

'Sit down, Hillbeam,' said Inspector Havelock, lazily. 'The house is surrounded.'

Muttering, Jimmy Hillbeam slumped in his seat, his eyes shifting around the room.

'We'll start with the will,' said Katherine. 'Mr Strutt, could you remind me whose legacies had increased in the will you read out?'

'Of course,' said Mr Strutt. 'Miss King, naturally. Then, ah, Miss Hillbeam and Tessie.'

'She was very kind to remember me in her will,' said

Tessie, indignantly.

'She was,' said Katherine. 'And *you* were very keen to remind me about Miss Quinton's herbal pillows. The ones which went missing.'

'They were lovely!' said Tessie. 'Sukey didn't ought to have taken them.' She looked accusingly at Sukey, who stared her out.

'No, she shouldn't have,' I said. 'But you were rather insistent about them. To the degree where we wondered why you wanted us to find them so badly. And when a speck of lavender was found in Miss Quinton's throat, the answer was clear. You wanted to suggest them as the murder weapon.'

'I did no such thing,' said Tessie, folding her arms.

'Well, it's very unlikely that *you* would have smothered her,' said Katherine. 'Imagine if anyone had caught the tweeny in her mistress's bedroom while she was resting.'

Tessie looked resentful, but said nothing.

'In any case,' Katherine added, 'why would you run the risk? All you had to do when Miss Quinton's medicine arrived was to tip most of it out and dilute the remainder with water.'

Tessie gasped. 'I never!'

Mrs Booth rounded on her. 'You said you was washing out an empty!'

Tessie's young face had hardened into sharp lines. 'And what about those *extra* tonics you made for her, Mrs B?'

'What about 'em?' But Mrs Booth's face had the foxy cast to it which I had seen briefly at Thirza Gregory's, when she was caught out over Abinhampton House.

'Gone for analysis,' Inspector Havelock said breezily. 'Now tell me about this pillow, Miss Caster.'

'I'd be delighted,' said Katherine. 'The pillow, of course, would be an excellent murder weapon; innocent-seeming, and already in the bedroom. So, who was most likely to use it? Whose presence in the bedroom would be acceptable when Miss Quinton was in bed?'

'Miss Taplow,' said Evangeline, studying her with a disgusted expression. 'Her companion.'

'Indeed,' said Katherine. 'And smothering a frail old lady would not require much strength.'

'But I had no reason to do it!' Miss Taplow cried. 'My bequest was reduced!'

'Ah, but you didn't know that,' I replied. 'Mr Latimer hadn't told you about the new will made at Christmas. The new will which he had instigated by hinting to Miss Quinton that you had guessed her little secret.'

Miss Taplow glared at Mr Latimer with utter hatred, which he paid back with a smug little smile.

'Miss Quinton decided not to dismiss you, since that would make you more likely to tell, but to punish you through her will.' Miss Taplow's hands clenched. 'Perhaps you detected a slight coolness in her manner eventually, and that, coupled with her refusal to die, made you determined to take matters into your own hands.'

'You have no proof whatsoever,' declared Miss Taplow, looking as if she smelt something unpleasant.

'But there's someone we haven't mentioned,' said Katherine. 'The person who, perhaps, has the most reason to wish Miss Quinton dead.'

Hillbeam twitched in her seat. 'Me?' she said, in a soft voice.

'I'm afraid so,' said Katherine. 'If Jonah Hillbeam hadn't asked us to find his family, we would never have known. Your sister worked here too, didn't she? And she ran away one day, and was never heard of again.'

'That's right,' murmured Hillbeam, in a voice dry and rustling as a dead leaf.

'And you knew no more till Miss Taplow came to be Miss Quinton's companion. She never liked you. She called you lazy and shiftless, and you never knew why. Yet what could you do, except put up with it?'

Hillbeam seemed to be sinking under the weight of the memory.

'Until one day you asked her, and it all came out. About the maid who had worked at Miss Taplow's family home for a short time before collapsing, and who had caused so much trouble. A housemaid called Hillbeam, Ruby she thought, who the doctor said had died of childbed fever. Imagine the morals, and the deceit!'

Hillbeam's head could bow no lower.

'So you pieced it together — Miss Quinton's hatred of men, and disgust with women who encouraged them, your sister's disappearance, and the poor housemaid with almost the same name, who had died just after childbirth, years and years ago. And you told your brother.'

'*Ohhhh*,' wailed Hillbeam.

'Miss Quinton liked her port, and she tended to keep it to herself. You had seen the doctor's medicine, and you knew your mistress had a heart complaint. You knew the lore about foxgloves — what would be easier than to give Miss Quinton a little more medicine than she needed? But someone might check the medicine bottle if she died suddenly, and Miss Quinton often didn't bother to take her dose. She always had her port, though, so you opted to dose her regularly till it took effect. The poison itself would have to be made off the premises, possibly by someone who knew a little of such things —' Katherine's eyes fell on Jimmy. 'But it proved surprisingly useful when more poison was required to try and get two persistent women off the trail.'

'I didn't know about that,' said Hillbeam, half to herself.

'I didn't think you did,' said Katherine. 'Any experienced parlourmaid would know that sending a bottle of poisoned port to two women wouldn't work, since they would be unlikely to share it in the office. However a working man who wasn't in service, and didn't drink (as evidenced by the temperance hotel you stayed at in London), might well make that mistake.'

The silence was broken by a long, satisfied sigh from Inspector Havelock. 'So who should I arrest first?' he asked.

'We can't be certain of who actually murdered Henrietta Quinton,' I said. 'Jimmy Hillbeam sent the port which poisoned Miss Caster's husband, which you can count as attempted murder, of course. And several of the rest of them have condemned each other out of their own mouths.' I sighed. 'If only our office hadn't been burgled.'

'Oh I wouldn't worry, Miss Fleet,' said the Inspector. 'Acting on the information which you passed me beforehand, officers with search warrants have been sent to the homes of all seven suspects. I daresay we'll find something before too long.'

'I daresay,' said Katherine. 'If you'd worked together you would probably have got away with it. As it turns out you've exposed each other, and — I suspect in several cases — signed your own death warrants.'

'Not me,' said Sukey, with defiance. Her lip curled as she surveyed her companions. 'To think, Miss Taplow, that *you* looked down on *me*.'

'Inspector Havelock, I'd appreciate it if you'd take these — people — to the police station,' said Evangeline. Her eyes flashed, and her cheeks were flushed. 'I do not want them in my house any longer.'

'I don't blame you, Miss King,' said the inspector, getting to his feet. 'I don't blame you at all. Now then!' he barked, startling everyone. 'Outside with you, and no funny business. Don't make me cuff you all together and walk you through the village.'

Eventually the front door closed behind the last person. Evangeline sank into the nearest chair and put her face in her hands. 'It's finished,' she said. 'It's over at last.'

'And you did wonderfully,' said Katherine, putting an arm around her.

'May I come in?' asked Moss, from the hall.

Evangeline's hands came down, and while she looked very serious, her eyes were dry. 'Of course you may.'

Katherine moved aside, and Moss took Evangeline in his arms.

'I've just realised something,' she said, looking up at

him. 'I said "my house". It's never felt like mine before. But I think I meant it.'

Mr Strutt coughed and made for the door, and Katherine and I followed.

'I'm so glad that's over,' I whispered. 'What an utter *mess* of a case!'

'It was,' said Katherine. 'But we did it. We solved it, and we probably prevented another murder, too. Oh, and one more thing.'

'What?'

Katherine put her hands on her rather obvious stomach. 'Baby was kicking like anything all the way through. He loved every minute of it.' She grinned. 'Perhaps he'll join the business!'

'Perhaps he will.' I grinned back. 'For now, let's return to Hazelgrove. Lunch is calling me.'

Katherine rolled her eyes. 'When *isn't* it, Connie?'

I considered a retort, but I was too happy to be snappish. 'At dinner time, my dear.' And we giggled as we linked arms to stroll back to Hazelgrove.

Chapter 27
Katherine

An unusually wet November had turned into a December so mild that Connie could put fresh primroses on the party tea-table for Bee's second birthday.

Only a few days later the wind became so bitter and the frosts so severe that despite the sniggers of the young, older people said the Thames would freeze as it had so many years before. In Berkshire, Hazelgrove stood surrounded by snow and Lion House lay dormant, while Evangeline and Moss planned its refurbishment prior to their June wedding.

Now it was a few days before Christmas. Seven of us sat around the dinner table in what was now Moss's house. Earlier Evangeline and Moss had been flicking through pattern books choosing wallpaper. Or at least Evangeline had been. Moss had simply stared at her with a daft expression on his face, accepting her choices. It was duller than the way James and I were approaching the same problem for ourselves, but a great deal more peaceful.

'I can't believe Katherine and James have decided to move house in January, two months before a baby is due,' said Margaret, sipping her sherry. 'Aren't they ridiculous, Connie?'

Connie, who had already told me her view on the matter, simply said. 'What else is there to do after New Year? Provided it doesn't actually snow in London and assuming the baby doesn't come early, everything will be fine.' Her sarcasm was almost tangible.

'It won't snow properly in London,' scoffed Albert, as the consommé was cleared and the mulled wine sorbet put before us. 'Those days have long gone.' He waved his spoon. 'All the smoke heats the air. Wonderful thing.'

'We're only moving two doors down from the apartment,' I argued. 'We needn't rush. I do wish everyone wouldn't fuss so. I would just prefer not to have to manhandle a perambulator up and down stairs. Or,' catching Connie's disapproving eye, 'expect the nursemaid to.'

'I hope we shall be able to get home tomorrow,' said Evangeline. 'I mean my home, I mean…' Blushing, she looked so pretty in the lamplight, her ruby droplet earrings reflecting the decorations on the table, the pearls sparkling in her dark hair. Moss was drinking every inch of her in. She flushed deeper as she looked at me. 'Not that it isn't lovely to be staying with you and James, of course. But I want Moss to see Hazelgrove at Christmas. You know how magical it is. Coming home after the midnight service with all the stars and the frost, to the house full of candlelight — there is nothing so wonderful in the world. I just hope that people in the village will speak to me.' She bit her lip.

'Don't worry,' said James. 'No-one has any complaint against you. Miss Quinton won't be mourned, but people don't like cheats or murderers among them either. After his arrest, a man in the village mentioned someone who'd crossed Jimmy Hillbeam and subsequently died unexpectedly, then someone else remembered something similar. Still rivers run deep, they say. It's only poor Keziah they pitied. Bullied from a child, they said. For all Jimmy's righteous indignation about Miss Quinton putting Ruth out of doors, I suspect the girl would have got short shrift from her brother too.'

'Poor Keziah,' said Evangeline. 'Do you really think the shame killed her?'

Margaret nodded. 'A-d-rforester believes so anyway.'

'Adderforester?' said Connie and I together.

'Dr Forester,' clarified Margaret with dignity. 'We correspond. About medicine.'

'Do you now?' I said.

She sipped her wine, her expression suspiciously neutral.

'At least her misery is over,' said Albert. 'Jonah has buried her decently with the remains of his mother and put up a proper headstone at last. The two sisters are slumbering together again, just as they did that last night before Ruth ran away.'

'I bet Tessie won't hang,' said Moss, coming out of his reverie to hand his half-finished sorbet to the maid. 'And that weasel Latimer will get away scot-free somehow. As for Mrs Booth, with her conviction for running an illegal still from that Gerrard Street restaurant in 1878, her chances of proving she didn't know how to distil herbs are very slim. You had a lucky escape, Margaret. To think she could have been your cook when you marry the mysterious Alexander.'

'Very funny, Moss,' said Margaret. 'Talking of romance —'

'The point is,' Moss interrupted as the beef Wellington was placed before him, 'murder can't go unpunished simply because the victim was unpopular. Evangeline was wonderful.'

'Are we wonderful too?' I whispered to Connie.

'We can't possibly compete,' she whispered back.

Margaret tried again. 'As I was saying —'

'What say after this nosh we sing carols?' said Albert, comparing his portion with James's, deciding he had the larger, and tucking in. 'Evangeline can play the piano and we'll see which of the ladies can do the best descant. I suppose Little Meg as the mere child should be the highest-pitched.'

Margaret glowered at him. 'I shall be twenty-one the day after these fools move house.' She jerked her head at me and James. 'An adult. Thereafter, anyone calling me Meg can expect trouble.'

Perhaps only I knew that under her bluster she felt sorry for Frank Taplow but, not loving him, was powerless to help. I wondered if Alexander Forester might be different.

I squeezed her hand, and she glanced at my stomach and

smiled. The baby was stretching and the black silk of my skirt moved as a foot or an elbow pushed against me.

'What's it like?' she whispered.

'Very uncomfortable,' I murmured. 'Despite what Connie says, I can't see how I can possibly get any larger. My ribs are getting bruised already, I'm sure. You do know we'd like you to live with us rather than go back to Fulham, don't you? Father doesn't seem to mind providing we visit, and Ada is determined to stay on with me because she doesn't trust anyone else to cook properly. I promise I won't ask too many questions if you're late home or want to invite people round.'

Margaret snorted. 'You can promise, but I know you will. All the same, thank you. I'd like to stay. Father and I do so annoy each other, and besides —'

'So now the baby's birth is so close, Katherine,' said Moss, 'I take it you and Connie will give up being Caster and Fleet? You'll have gone out on a triumph. And without meaning to be indelicate, you won't be able to steal cabs or climb out of windows for a while.'

'That's for us to decide,' said Connie. 'We do have cases still on the books. Easy ones. But after Christmas, even if no-one tells Katherine to stop, I shall. There's still a nursemaid to hire and things to buy and more importantly, rest to be had.'

'For both of you,' said Albert sternly, then patted his stomach. 'That was delicious. I have to say your menu is a lot less likely to cause dyspepsia than Pa's was. What's next?'

'Conservative pudding, vanilla and almond blancmange

or pêche Melba,' said the maid, indicating the sideboard. 'Which would you like, Mr Albert sir?'

Albert pondered. 'Perhaps a bit of each?'

'Oh, honestly,' said Connie. 'For shame. I'll never be able to think of pêche Melba again without thinking of Mrs Booth.'

'Nor me,' I said. I didn't feel like anything else to eat. There wasn't room. I leaned behind James, who was talking to Albert. 'Connie, when I'm back from Hazelgrove, would you shout at me if I had one last day in the office before the baby comes? I'd like to sit there for a while, feeling like I know what I'm doing. I'm starting to feel a little scared.'

'I didn't think you were scared of anything.'

'I'm scared of everything. I'm just good at pretending. And all this nursery nonsense —'

'It's not the nursery that worries you, is it?'

'No.'

'When the men take the port, we'll talk in the drawing room.'

Moss cleared his throat and tapped his wine glass. 'I think a toast is in order before the stilton comes out. It's a shame Uncle Roderick wasn't able to join us.'

'He had a prior engagement,' I explained. 'Although he's missed a fine feast. Thank you, Moss.'

'He has indeed,' said James. 'And now that I am feeling mellow, it's a shame he's not here to talk us into somnolence. It would mean we wouldn't have to listen to you ladies caterwauling carols.'

The doorbell rang.

'Oh dear, a telegram?' said Evangeline. 'Whatever's wrong?'

A loud voice sounded in the hall and before we knew it the door burst open bringing a blast of freezing air, Father and Miss Thirza Gregory.

'Aha! I thought we might find you here!' boomed Father, as if he'd found the source of the Nile. 'We have come fresh from the Savoy with a basket of Sweetmeats, Ghost Stories to tell you by the fireside and News! Not, of course, in that order!'

It was amazing how you could hear the capital letters. Father waved his arms even while the parlourmaid was trying to divest him of his frosty overcoat and basket, nearly knocking her cap off. He ushered Miss Gregory forward, put his arm around her and suddenly the two of them looked as if they were about five years old and had been caught stealing apples.

'I'm not sure whose permission to ask,' he said. 'So I'll ask my daughters. Margaret may have guessed already. I've asked Miss Gregory to be my wife. Will you give us your blessing?'

Margaret and I grinned at each other, then rose and kissed them both fondly.

'Of course we do, Father,' I said. 'Take a seat — we were about to make a toast. Now we can make two.'

'Best make it three,' said Father, as an extra chair was brought and a large portion of conservative pudding put before him. 'It's started to snow outside. Apparently we're going to have a white Christmas and whiter January. Just as well there's nothing important happening.'

DEMERAY & SWIFT FAMILY TREES. CHARACTERS IN ITALICS ARE DECEASED. CHARACTERS IN GREY DO NOT TAKE PART IN THIS BOOK.

LAMONT & KING FAMILY TREES. CHARACTERS IN ITALICS ARE DECEASED. CHARACTERS IN GREY DO NOT TAKE PART IN THIS BOOK.

Lamont Family

Maurice — m — *Charlotte Demeroy (d)* (DEMERAY FAMILY TREE)

Children of Maurice & Charlotte:
- Maurice (Moss)
- *Henry (d)*
- Terence — m — Elizabeth
- John — m — Judith
- Antonia
- Douglas
- Albert — m — Constance (Connie) (SWIFT FAMILY TREE)

Children of Albert & Constance:
- Beatrix (Bee)
- George

King Family

Edwin King — m — Dorothea Forbes

Children of Edwin & Dorothea:
- *Edwin (d)*
- *Isaac (d)*
- *Dora (d)*
- *Angelina (d)*
- *Reuben (d)*
- Evangeline
- James — m — Katherine (DEMERAY FAMILY TREE)

Acknowledgements

First of all, thank you to our beta readers — Ruth Cunliffe, Christine Downes, Stephen Lenhardt, and Val Portelli. As ever we gave ourselves plenty to do in not too much time, and you all helped tremendously. Thank you so much! Any errors remaining in the book are of course the responsibility of the authors.

This book didn't require quite as much research as some of Caster & Fleet's other adventures; however, there are a couple of sources we'd like to mention:

A is for Arsenic: The Poisons of Agatha Christie by Kathryn Harkup (Bloomsbury, 2015): https://www.goodreads.com/book/show/23848320-a-is-for-arsenic.

The Victorian Web, a huge repository and source for all things Victorian: http://www.victorianweb.org.

Victorian London, a website full of useful primary sources, curated by Lee Jackson: http://www.victorianlondon.org/index-2012.htm.

If you think we made up the strange weather in the last

chapter — we didn't! https://en.wikipedia.org/wiki/Winter_of_1894–95_in_the_United_Kingdom.

And of course, thank you for reading! We hope you've enjoyed the latest adventure of our dynamic duo, and if you could leave the book a short review — or a star rating — on Amazon or Goodreads we'd be very grateful.

Font and image credits

Fonts:

Main cover font: Birmingham Titling by Paul Lloyd (freeware):
https://www.fontzillion.com/fonts/paul-lloyd/birmingham.

Classic font: Libre Baskerville Italic by Impallari Type (http://www.impallari.com): https://www.fontsquirrel.com/fonts/libre-baskerville License — SIL Open Font License v.1.10: http://scripts.sil.org/OFL

Vector graphics:

Bottle (decolourised): Figured flask by J.R. Robinson & Sons, part of the collection of the Metropolitan Museum of Art: https://images.metmuseum.org/CRDImages/ad/original/DP207128.jpg. Open access: public domain.

Lavender (cropped and decolourised): Lavender Flower by crepesuzette at https://pixabay.com/photos/lavender-flower-purple-2395071/. License: public domain.

Horse and carriage vignette by Open Clipart Vectors at

https://pixabay.com/vectors/buggy-carriage-horse-horse-drawn-2027141/. License: public domain.

Letters vignette (decolourised and contrast levels altered) at https://pixabay.com/photos/old-letters-mail-old-stamps-2238537/. License: public domain.

Cover created using GIMP image editor: www.gimp.org.

About Paula Harmon

At her first job interview, Paula Harmon answered the question 'where do you see yourself in 10 years' with 'writing', as opposed to 'progressing in your company.' She didn't get that job. She tried teaching and realised the one thing the world did not need was another bad teacher. Somehow or other she subsequently ended up as a civil servant and if you need to know a form number, she is your woman.

Her short stories include dragons, angst ridden teenagers, portals and civil servants (though not all in the same story — yet). Perhaps all the life experience was worth it in the end.

Paula is a Chichester University English graduate. She is married with two children and lives in Dorset. She is currently working on a thriller, a humorous murder mystery and something set in an alternative universe. She's wondering where the housework fairies are, because the house is a mess and she can't think why.

Website: www.paulaharmondownes.wordpress.com
Amazon author page: http://viewAuthor.at/PHAuthorpage

Goodreads: https://goodreads.com/paula_harmon
Twitter: https://twitter.com/PaulaHarmon789

Books by Paula Harmon

Murder Britannica
When Lucretia's plan to become very rich is interrupted by a series of unexpected deaths, local wise-woman Tryssa starts to ask questions.

The Cluttering Discombobulator
Can everything be fixed with duct tape? Dad thinks so. The story of one man's battle against common sense and the family caught up in the chaos around him.

Kindling
Is everything quite how it seems? Secrets and mysteries, strangers and friends. Stories as varied and changing as British skies.

The Advent Calendar
Christmas as it really is, not the way the hype says it is (and sometimes how it might be) — stories for midwinter.

The Quest
In a parallel universe, dragons are used for fuel and the people who understand them are feared as spies and traitors. Can two estranged sisters, descended from the dragon-people, save the country from revolution?

Weird and Peculiar Tales (with Val Portelli)
Short stories from this world and beyond.

About Liz Hedgecock

Liz Hedgecock grew up in London, England, did an English degree, and then took forever to start writing. After several years working in the National Health Service, some short stories crept into the world. A few even won prizes. Then the stories began to grow longer . . .

Now Liz travels between the nineteenth and twenty-first centuries, murdering people. To be fair, she does usually clean up after herself.

Liz's reimaginings of Sherlock Holmes, her Pippa Parker cozy mystery series, and *Bitesize*, a collection of flash fiction, are available in ebook and paperback.

Liz lives in Cheshire with her husband and two sons, and when she's not writing or child-wrangling you can usually find her reading, messing about on Twitter, or cooing over stuff in museums and art galleries. That's her story, anyway, and she's sticking to it.

Website/blog: http://lizhedgecock.wordpress.com
Facebook: http://www.facebook.com/lizhedgecockwrites
Twitter: http://twitter.com/lizhedgecock
Goodreads: https://www.goodreads.com/lizhedgecock

Books by Liz Hedgecock

Short stories
The Secret Notebook of Sherlock Holmes
Bitesize

Halloween Sherlock series (novelettes)
The Case of the Snow-White Lady
Sherlock Holmes and the Deathly Fog
The Case of the Curious Cabinet

Sherlock & Jack series (novellas)
A Jar Of Thursday
Something Blue
A Phoenix Rises

Mrs Hudson & Sherlock Holmes series (novels)
A House Of Mirrors
In Sherlock's Shadow

Pippa Parker Mysteries (novels)
Murder At The Playgroup
Murder In The Choir
A Fete Worse Than Death
Murder In The Meadow

Caster & Fleet Mysteries (with Paula Harmon)
The Case of the Black Tulips
The Case of the Runaway Client
The Case of the Deceased Clerk
The Case of the Masquerade Mob
The Case of the Fateful Legacy

Printed in Great Britain
by Amazon